The Gap

by

Cristina Fernández Cubas

Translated by

Kathryn Phillips-Miles & Simon Deefholts

The Clapton Press

Cristina Fernández Cubas (Arenys de Mar, 1945) is an award-winning Spanish writer and journalist. She has published several novels, a biography of Emilia Pardo Bazán and six collections of short stories. Her most recent collection of short stories earned her the Premio Nacional de Literatura and has been published in English translation under the title *Nona's Room.*

El año de Gracia © 1985 Cristina Fernández Cubas
The Gap Year or The Year of Grace © 2022 Kathryn Phillips-Miles & Simon Deefholts

Cover design by Jenny Fell

First published 2022 by:
THE CLAPTON PRESS LTD,
38 Thistlewaite Road, London E5

ISBN: 978-1-913693-14-5

Support for the translation of this book was provided by:

AC/E
ACCIÓN CULTURAL
ESPAÑOLA

In memory of
Amalia Cubas Moreno

Part I

1

Although I spent the best years of my life with my back turned against the world, devoting my time to studying theology and learning dead languages, I have only myself to blame for the unspeakable misfortunes I have suffered.

I entered the seminary of my own free will, ignoring the pleas and advice of my family, battling against their fierce anticlericalism and brimming with pride every time my father took the trouble to send me a letter to remind me that he had resolved to write me out of his will. When I heard the news of his death, however, I was overwhelmed by a strange sense of unease. I didn't attach much importance to this at first and put my distress down to the loss that I'd just suffered and I tried to immerse myself in my favourite occupations: reading and studying. But the irresistible charm of the seminary's magnificent library quickly faded away. Books piled up unread on the desk in my cell, and my daily translations from Greek—a task at which I used to excel—were peppered, with alarming frequency, with clumsy, inexcusable errors. Now that my father was dead, the monastic life felt like nothing more than a whole litany of ridiculous sacrifices. Enticing rays of sunlight shone through the refectory windows, the cold winter had given way to an intoxicating spring, and in the garden there were buds on the rose bushes and the almond trees were beginning to blossom. I felt as if the world was about to throw a magnificent banquet and it was my fate to be excluded. For the first time in many years, my body had taken on a life of its own. It demanded fresh air, the sea, new and exciting experiences.

The atmosphere of the old granite building was beginning to suffocate me. In the mornings I would walk in the garden, munching on apples, trampling over seedlings, breaking into song or into a skip and a jump like a small schoolboy whenever I thought that no one could see me. In the evenings I would open my cell window, gaze up at the stars and, because my room was so small, bang the back of my neck in a painful reproach.

My malaise didn't go unnoticed by my fellow students and neither did my odd early-morning behaviour escape the eagle eye of the brother who acted as doorkeeper. But there was little I could do to help myself. A strange sort of inebriation permeated everything I did and, when the Rector amicably told me he was surprised by my behaviour, all I could do was formulate questions to which I had already found the answers, in private, some time ago. How can you renounce something that you know nothing about? What value could there be in the self-denial of an inexperienced boy? Who exactly was it, to whom I was so keen to show my contempt for worldly trifles? Now that I no longer had a target audience, my heroic act had become one of dereliction, my courage a mere retreat. Finally, on the morning of 7th June 1980, I said farewell to the seminary with the same resolve as when I'd abandoned the secular world, seven years earlier.

2

Grace delivered a warning shot straight away. She was tired, sleepy, didn't have the slightest interest in my life at the seminary and she told me that, from now on, I was to stop asking her about her husband. It was nobody's business but theirs whether he had left her or whether she had made such a frivolous decision. And then she invited me to lunch. A light lunch, which was as big a surprise as my visit. She didn't add the words "inconvenient" or "tedious" and I didn't wait around to give her the opportunity. I'd got to my feet and was about to leave when my sister gave me a big smile, which was what I least expected.

'Now, I've no idea why, but this reminds me of the last time we saw each other . . .'

Grace was still an attractive woman, despite the fact that age had accentuated her sharp features and her eyes no longer shone as they once had. But then, I thought to myself, I probably didn't look the same to her, either. Our last conversation had taken place years earlier, in the seminary gardens, and my attitude then (as she reminded me now with a enigmatic smile) could not have been less polite or more inappropriate. On that occasion I thanked her for her interest in me but, at the same time, making up some ridiculous excuse, I begged her to stop visiting me. The truth was I was ashamed of her, with her bright red lipstick and her insistence on turning up in the most showy and outlandish clothes; ashamed of the pungent trail of perfume that would linger, for hours after she'd left, in the halls, corridors and cloisters. Grace took it very well and never came back. But now, here I was, faced with the same bright red lips and the same perfume and I was the one feeling stupid and inadequate. Her eyes took in my well-worn black shirt, carried on down to my grey trousers and settled, with no attempt to disguise her irritation, on the pointed toe of one of my patent leather shoes. 'My God!' was all she said.

That very day I moved back into our former family home. After a lunch punctuated with periods of silence and heavy sighs, it was actually Grace who made the decision so authoritatively that she gave me no chance to answer back and there was no room for anyone to disagree, least of all me. It was (and I remember this as clear as day) a short while after I had finally managed, inexpertly and with much stuttering, to make her understand that I had resolved to live in the secular world. Grace looked at me in astonishment and said, 'That's better. That's much better.' Then she smiled at me again and, for a brief moment, her eyes shone as they used to in the old days. But I didn't have the chance to relive scenes from our childhood, share memories or even strike up a friendly, everyday conversation. My sister stood up straight away. 'I'll show you to your room,' she said. And, feeling like a child despite the fact that I was twenty-four years old, I followed her down the long corridor without a word, not daring to object, reject her offer or even simply say thank you.

It didn't take me long to realise that, lurking behind her offer and her fleeting moment of happiness, my sister had a plan for me and there was no room for mercy or compassion. Grace had determined to re-educate me according to her ways, and the mysterious disappearance of my shoes the next morning, quickly followed by the rest of my sparse wardrobe a few days later, would be nothing less than a subtle prelude to a long list of remonstrances and words of advice. Fortunately, it never occurred to me to doubt her intentions or my destiny.

For the first few weeks I didn't have any time to think about the life I was leaving behind, since I was fully immersed in the one I was now being forced to share. My sister took me to the best restaurants, invited me to the latest shows . . . But however much I tried, I couldn't escape the long, tedious parties where she was in her element, talking non-stop and drinking like a fish. After those soirées I would try in vain to seek refuge in the tranquillity of my bedroom. Because there was always a blunder, an inappropriate comment, some remark or a pause which Grace would never fail to point out breezily as if it hadn't been me who'd put my foot in it, as if she were not always on the look out for my *faux pas*. Sometimes she didn't even bother to put into words what she could say just with a glare. After one of those accusing looks I had no choice but to learn my lesson. From then on I would have to walk with my head held high, refrain from interlocking my fingers and abstain from all the mannerisms I'd picked up in the seminary, if I didn't want to make a display that was just as inappropriate as a pungent trail of perfume inside an old granite building. Everything was starting to become clearer and clearer between the two of us.

However, despite my growing affection for Grace, and although she seemed happy and excited about my strange re-education, there was one uncomfortable issue which, right from the start, put a strain on us living under the same roof: I didn't have a penny. The small inheritance which my father had not been able to deny me wasn't available in ready cash, and I couldn't hide from the fact that, sooner or later, I'd have to find a job and relinquish the comfort of my sister's warm embrace. I didn't know how to broach it and, although I tried to several times, Grace always managed to change the subject, suddenly remembering a pressing engagement which couldn't be postponed, or getting into a fierce argument with the cook, the chauffeur or the concierge. I guessed, however, that she was nursing an idea or hatching a new plot. For several days I noticed her shuffling papers and files, talking things over with her agent, drawing up budgets and closely following the foreign exchange rate. Then one afternoon she asked me, 'Do you know any foreign languages, apart from Latin?' and I said 'yes.' For a brief moment, a triumphant smile swept away the tiredness from her face.

That night we had dinner in a quiet restaurant. It was hot but, at her request, I wore a dark brown velvet suit. For my benefit, Grace wore her most modest outfit: a green dress with a red petunia print. We were both jubilant and in high spirits although I still had no idea what my sister was planning. It was all a little emotional. Because that night Grace had insisted on taking us back to our old playroom, to childhood dreams of adventures that we'd never managed to fulfil, to distant summers (and this I particularly remembered) when it seemed like we were the closest friends in the world. 'No, time hasn't passed,' she said. 'Everything must carry on exactly the same.' And, although I didn't really understand what she meant, it made me think back to Grace in her youth, radiant with smooth skin, full of life and brimming with joy. Stupidly, I was scared to look up at her.

'Back then,' she continued, 'you were almost as handsome as you are now. You had girlfriends by the dozen, do you remember?'

I shrugged my shoulders. The truth was I couldn't remember. But I suspected that she was going to introduce me to someone or that, at some point, the nondescript face of some forgotten girlfriend from my youth would appear at the door. I heard her say, 'just pretend that time hasn't passed,' several times and I surprised myself by ordering a brandy.

'It's all going to be more difficult for you here,' she said after a pause. 'Think about it. You deserve a breather. Travel a bit, sort yourself out . . .'

She paused again as if to catch her breath and added, 'That's why I've decided to make amends for how unfairly our father treated you. This is my offer: you can have a year, as a present from me.'

Then she reached over for my brandy which I hadn't even touched as I was so completely bowled over, and knocked it back in one.

Grace had the rare gift of being able to give someone a present without causing any offence, hiding her generosity under the guise of being outlandish or capricious, making light of the way she was gradually solving my problems before I'd even identified them. I loved her more than ever and at that moment the image of a tender young girl which I'd been nurturing nostalgically a few minutes earlier no longer held my interest. I adored her as the mature woman who was now smiling at me expectantly from the other side of the table, with those heavily veined hands that softly gestured to the waiter that she was desperate for another drink, with that face lined with premature wrinkles and hidden disappointments. I felt an urge to throw myself into her arms. But I didn't do anything. My sister insisted on maintaining her distance.

'A gap year?' I said finally, and immediately felt embarrassed in case I had spoken too soon.

'Call it whatever you like,' she replied with feigned indifference.

And then I could contain myself no longer. I felt an embarrassing lump in my throat, my eyes brimmed with tears and I was seized by a curious sensation that was both delightful and ridiculous at the same time. When I took her hands in mine, all I could manage to stammer out was, 'I will always think of it as *your* year . . . the *Year of Grace*.'

My sister's only response was to extract a pair of sunglasses from her handbag and hold them out to me, insistently.

3

I have to confess that I would have liked Grace to have come to the station on 1st September, the morning I caught the train to Paris. I waited for her to show up right until the last moment; she didn't and when I think about it there was no good reason to expect her to. Now, looking back, I understand that her absence had been carefully and astutely planned. Grace didn't want to display the fragility which I so wanted to see in her, or to become the diminutive figure on the platform waving farewell to her loved one with a brave smile. Maybe it was because of her visceral hatred of anything to do with emotion or feeling. Maybe also because her extraordinary intuition told her that we would never meet again for the rest of our lives.

But, right then, how could I complain about my good luck? I still have a clear and unforgettable memory of the first few months of my time in Paris. I'd found myself a decent place to stay, Grace's cheques arrived like clockwork and my only day to day concern was the delightful task of deciding what to do and how to fill the next twenty-four hours. I was absolutely free and that rare gift, together with the fact that I never attempted to present myself as a man of the world (which I knew I wasn't) provided me with unforgettable experiences and friendships. I soon realized that my insecurity, hidden behind a foreign language, was seen as politeness and my reticence as discretion. I knew how to make people like me and I intended to take full advantage of the strong element of surprise that my education held for anyone who was unaware of my past.

I'd discovered a friendly café a few blocks away from my attic room. I liked the atmosphere, the groups of men and women who were regulars, the snippets of conversation I pretended not to overhear. I went there every afternoon at the same time and, whenever possible, I tried to sit at the same table next to the window. It was a place with a stable clientele and before long I too became a regular. One day the waiter, looking over my shoulder at the book I was reading, asked me if I was Greek. I said 'no' in a loud enough voice for everyone at the adjacent tables to hear. Another day, as if by mistake, I left a carefully chosen edition of Ovid's *Metamorphoses*, in the original Latin, next to my coffee cup. When I went back for it, a couple of students were leafing through the book. Just as I'd intended, tongues started wagging. Within a few days I was no longer the quiet man by the window and I had become "the dapper young man who, strangely, only reads books in Latin and Greek." My visiting card had been left on the table.

Liberated from the task of having to pretend, I tried to immerse myself in reading, as I had once done in the solitude of my cell. But I didn't quite manage it. Everything that I had planned with more than a touch of fantasy now came true with mathematical precision. Soon the timid exchange of greetings with the group closest to my table turned into warm, animated conversations. I made friends, I was admired and, much sooner than I had expected, I put Homer, Ovid and Herodotus to one side and began to live. One afternoon I met Yasmine.

I owe Yasmine almost as much as I owe Grace and, perhaps because of that, I behaved towards her like a conceited, ungrateful student. Yasmine opened up her heart to me and I was infected by her boundless happiness. With Yasmine by my side, I enjoyed the best days of my rediscovered youth. I found her job really fascinating. She would turn up at the café with her Leica M-3 (from which she was inseparable) and a portfolio bulging with contact prints and an enormous handbag full of all kinds of exotic, strange objects. Back then, I hardly knew anything about women and handbags, and Yasmine's sudden incursion into my life put paid to any vague travel plans or story book dreams of adventures. I never asked her how old she was and neither, right at the beginning, did I really care. Yasmine was a slender, attractive woman who loved her job and was brimming over with sweetness and light. She could fudge her way through six or seven different languages with great skill, enough to find her way around any spot in the world, access impenetrable places and capture, apparently effortlessly, just the right photo, never to be repeated. She worked for an important daily in Paris and, almost without realizing it, I found myself sharing her job, her happiness and her bed.

But I didn't know how to enjoy caresses or devotion. A dangerous and disturbing feeling threatened to take control of me for the second time in a very short period. I would kiss Yasmine and my mind would be flooded by all the kisses that the world had to offer me which, by choosing hers, I chose to reject. I loved Yasmine and I was gripped by the fear that she would be not only my first great love but also my last. The constant travelling that her job forced on us began to wear me down. I was living her life, Yasmine's life, in very much the same way as, months earlier, my sister Grace had assertively taken control of mine. Yasmine and Grace. Who were they really? Gradually I began to harbour an uncomfortable suspicion that our meeting in the café had not been by chance and that my display of eccentricities had not been as effective as I had naively believed. Yasmine and Grace must have known each other, they were friends or, even worse, they were in cahoots.

These suspicions were, of course, improbable, but the

vast quantities of alcohol which I had begun to enjoy consuming in those days lent them an unquestionable semblance of reality. Yasmine, although curious and pushy, never asked me where my money came from and neither had Grace, in her letters, ever shown the slightest interest in the reason for my change of address or asked me what my new accommodation was like. These clues could not have been more flimsy but they were enough to liberate me from Yasmine's arms without too much self-reproach. In fact, I was becoming conceited and arrogant. I attributed my good luck to my personal qualities; Yasmine's love to my irresistible attraction; even Grace's generosity suddenly seemed to me to be a simple act of reparation and justice. During that emotional time which I think back on now with a certain sense of shame, I ended up believing that I was enveloped in an aura to which, in my naivety, I attributed protective qualities.

However, while my mind was excited by the thought of change, breaking up with Yasmine wasn't easy for me. I started going on fewer trips with her, I relished her absence, revelled in reunions and humiliated her with a long list of affairs that have left no trace on my memory. I left her for good in Saint-Malo.

I don't know whether everyone who dreams of adventure has felt a similar fascination to mine as I strolled along the quayside at Saint-Malo under the weak March sun. A westerly wind was blowing and the masts of the sailing boats danced together in an unforgettable harmony. All the books which I had read so avidly in earlier times now gathered in my memory, in no particular order or arrangement. I remembered Morgan, the Lion of Damascus, Long John Silver, Captain Nemo, Gordon Pym. I felt all the uneasiness of young Jim Hawkins from the Admiral Benbow Inn anticipating his first voyage. One of the boats caught my attention. It must have been twelve metres long and was probably the oldest and least valuable one there, but there was something about the well-cared for, shiny masts and decks which spoke of a close bond between the vessel and its owner. I paused to imagine the secret history of that old relic. If I half-closed my eyes or blinked or ignored the ostentatious yachts beside it, that simple boat took on all the majesty of a pirate ship. It had been freshly painted in black gloss and a somewhat mature man, hanging on to some ropes and dressed in a garish red bomber jacket, was putting the finishing touches to the name on the prow. I went up close and read: *PROVIDENCE*. But that's not the only thing I did. I liked the look of the man, his bushy beard infused me with confidence, and my conceitedness and arrogance took care of the rest.

I'll spare the details of the first few talks I had with the captain of the *Providence* because I consider them unimportant. I'll just mention that I used all my charms, fell back on the most tried and tested banalities and drew, as usual, on my childish display of knowledge combined with traces of shyness and a genuine curiosity about the boat's features and the purpose of various instruments. By the time evening fell, I deliberately forgot about my date with Yasmine and I invited my new friend for a drink in the bar on the quayside. I discovered that he was setting sail for Glasgow in a couple of days, that his name was Jean and that he was known affectionately as *"Captain Jean"* by his friends in every port the world over. I offered to help him make his final preparations and he accepted almost too happily and delightedly, something which would have given pause for thought to the most reckless of men. But I was angling for an invitation which didn't take long to materialise and I focussed all my efforts on that objective.

That night, when I got back to the hotel, I congratulated myself on my ingenuity, packed my things and left a note for Yasmine at reception, telling her I was leaving. "I'm going back to Paris," I wrote. "I'll call you in a few days." The message seemed a bit curt so I added, "Big hug." But the fact that I was lying to her didn't make me feel in the least bit uncomfortable. I wanted to live, to answer the call that the world was sending out to me, make up for my seven years of peaceful retreat at breakneck speed. The time had come to give up my life of caresses and soft linen, sisters and protectresses, and set off to sea. I didn't want to look back or reflect on what I was leaving behind. It was as if the real *Year of Grace* were beginning right there and then and, guided by all my childhood dreams, I prepared to set out on what I looked upon as the first episode of a great adventure. Afterwards, in Glasgow, the world at large or my own lucky star would be sure to present me with new horizons.

I moved to a cheap lodging house near the quay and, for the next few days, I gave Captain Jean all the help he needed. At no point did I listen to my instincts or take even one minute out of those eventful days to reflect on how surprisingly easy it had been to achieve my objective. Wasn't it true that Grace had helped me in such a way that I hadn't had any time to identify my own problems? And more to the point, hadn't I seduced Yasmine using the same charms? But the hard-working Captain wasn't in the least bit like sweet Yasmine and, while I put my heart and soul into tying down ropes, greasing the engine and jotting down in my notebook terms like "bowsprit", "binnacle" and "hawser", I noticed the Captain smiling to himself and counting his blessings that he'd come across such a strange bird. A naïve foreigner, a chatterbox, who was self-financing and, above all, had absolutely no idea about the most basic concepts of the art of navigation and the vagaries of the sea.

4

For the first few days on board the *Providence*, Captain Jean was kind and generous with his time, keen to teach me the secrets of sailing and turning a blind eye to my inevitable beginner's errors. I was flattered by how patiently he answered my questions and how he smiled understandingly as he watched me out of the corner of his eye writing everything down, or sketching pictures, in my brand new notebook. For my part, I tried to reciprocate with genuine admiration for him. For me, Captain Jean was like a character out of a novel, an old sea dog who didn't even need to open his mouth in order to convince me that his life had been full of danger and adventures; humanity and wisdom oozed from his every pore.

One evening, the Captain showed me a photograph of a magnificent looking Polynesian girl he'd known in Pago-Pago. As youngsters, they'd had a passionate affair, incurring the anger of Malbú, her authoritarian father. Of all the women he had known, it was definitely Maliba who had left the deepest impression on him and, even now, so many years later, he would occasionally wonder, after one or two tots of rum, whether it would have been more sensible to have renounced his love for the sea and ended his days in a little shack, being caressed by Maliba and spoiled by a dozen little olive-skinned children. He couldn't forget her cantankerous father, Malbú, either. On stormy days, a judicious blend of powerful herbs which only grow in Samoa, and a steel spear-tip, tempered in the heat of mysterious spells, were all he needed to remind himself of just how much hatred one Polynesian man whose honour has been offended can harbour. He showed me the impressive scar across his left thigh and I shuddered. A heavy swell made me drop my glass and a fair amount of alcohol spilled over Maliba's placid face. Much to my relief, the Captain scarcely batted an eyelid. He wiped the faded photograph with a cloth and said, 'A drop of rum will do her good.' Then, relegating Samoa to the depths of his memory, he transported me to the fascinating hustle and bustle of Singapore, Port-au-Prince and Dakar.

Whereas the Captain was all bonhomie and kindness, the same could not be said for Naguib, the deck hand, when it came to the smallest mistake on my part. My presence on board seemed to really irritate him. He didn't bother to answer any of my questions and, if I ever tried to be friendly, he would reject my best intentions with a cutting remark or an affected silence. While we were still in Saint-Malo, a few hours before setting sail, I saw him looking at me with his eyes full of pure animosity. But I didn't pay him much attention and, although I would have liked to grill Naguib about where he came from and hear him recounting tales of pharaohs, hieroglyphs and ancient tombs, I understood straight away that he didn't know much about all of that and, in any case, he didn't want anything to do with me. On one occasion, frustrated with my phrasebook Arabic, I added a flourish which I thought was a polite set phrase (*Kaifa háluka, ya sayíd?*). He looked at me in utter contempt. 'Don't even bother trying,' he said, and he turned his back on me.

I had learned not to pry into other people's lives and I ended up ignoring him. This was quite easy, despite how it looked. Naguib was a man of few words and, even if the *Providence* was not the best place to cut oneself off from someone else, with a small mental effort I managed to scale him down to the same level as a ship's log, a sextant or a lifeboat. I have no idea what image the Egyptian had mentally assigned to me, but I am pretty confident that it was nothing quite so benign.

In spite of all that, at the bottom of my heart I couldn't help but understand his attitude. He was an excellent sailor without a shadow of doubt. At night, when Naguib was in command of the *Providence*, the Captain never showed the slightest concern and spent his time sleeping, chatting to me or teaching me new things which I carefully noted down together with sketches and drawings. Naguib was a good man to have on board, he told me. Possibly the best, I concluded. That was the only way I could make sense of it all; why a man of Captain Jean's calibre would go on one of his trips with someone who had such limited conversation and appeal. What was more, his character helped me explain my own presence on board. This had not given me the slightest pause for thought on dry land but now, at the mercy of the laws of the sea, I began to feel my presence was both absurd and unnecessary.

As it turned out, I hadn't been of much help. I spent the first day being seasick and nauseous, and it was only my implacable appetite for learning that forced me to stay on my feet and hide my overwhelming discomfort from the others. It was my maiden voyage, my baptism at sea. The Captain understood and lost no time in advising me to move out of my narrow bunk and make myself comfortable in the cabin. Clearly, Captain Jean had not invited me to join them for my potential experience, but for my simple, friendly company. It was also clear that for Naguib, who found conversation irritating, I was nothing more than a hindrance or an obstacle to his enjoyment of a quiet life. However, a minor incident (at first, I didn't realize it was so significant) would very soon convince me to exercise extreme discretion and proceed with the utmost caution.

As I have mentioned, the first few days were character-ised by the Captain's kindness, the Egyptian's contempt and my (not always successful) attempts to fit in, provoking smiles from the former and irritated glances from the latter. We had left Saint-Malo early in the morning on 13th March. There was a north-westerly wind and we proceeded under sail, as Captain Jean had promised. On the third day, I was awoken by the humming of an engine. I was alone in the cabin, the temperature had dropped like a stone and I lazed for a while longer in the bunk before resolving to get up and put on whatever was closest to hand. I was reheating some coffee when the door burst open and a blast of icy wind snuffed out the flame on the paraffin stove. I immediately understood why I felt so stiff. I had a quick look at the door and was delighted to find that the handle had broken. I've always been fairly handy at carpentry jobs and that small mishap would give me the chance to feel useful all morning. I left the cabin to think over the task. That's when I heard them.

'Cardiff,' said Naguib.

'Glasgow,' said Captain Jean.

'Cardiff,' said Naguib.

A blast of wind hit me at the same time as a particularly emphatic, 'Glasgow.' I looked up. The two men were talking on deck and their voices sounded dry and tense.

'There are fast and comfortable trains to and from Cardiff,' said Naguib.

'And in Glasgow,' said the Captain with a roar, 'there's a

31

magnificent boatyard, as well as something much more important for you. Do I need to remind you?'

'OK,' the Egyptian shouted. 'We'll sail to Glasgow if that's what you want, Captain. But I won't put up with any more delays.'

Captain Jean, by way of response, punched the air.

I still didn't know if what I'd just heard had something to do with me and, in truth, there was nothing to seriously suggest that it did. So I went and found the toolbox, went back out on deck and, probably intending to give the impression of being contented and unconcerned, I decided to sing the only jolly song I could remember. The wind beat against my face and the first few bars were lost in the crashing waves. But I could still hear what they were saying.

'This isn't a pleasure trip,' the Egyptian said.

Just at that moment I dropped the toolbox. A saw, two set-squares and loads of nails in various sizes scattered in all directions. Some compartments hadn't come open and the tools rattled and clattered around inside. As I'd anticipated, the two men stopped talking. I went back to my singing, pretended to survey the damage and set about measuring the hinge, as if it were the most natural thing in the world. After a while I looked up and shouted, 'Good morning!' And then, pointing at the door, I added, 'It'll be all fixed in a couple of hours!' The Captain returned my greeting. I pretended not to hear him and carried on picking up the nails from the deck. I didn't dare look at Naguib. But I imagined he was standing still, in the same position as a few minutes earlier, his eyes bloodshot and bulging, his muscles tensed and his last words ('pleasure trip') filling the air with an unbearable sarcasm.

I spent the rest of the morning repairing the door, endeavouring to do a good job and reflecting on what had happened. Naguib's attitude towards the Captain didn't fit the role of a common deck hand used to receiving orders, carrying them out and being paid for it. 'But I won't put up with any more delays,' he'd said and, judging from his confident tone it wasn't the first time he'd spoken so arrogantly. He was definitely a good sailor, as I'd told myself again and again *ad nauseum*, but however good he was, that seemed irrelevant when it came to weighing up his behaviour, even conceding that the significance of the word 'delays' might include a reference to me and that I might be the only obstacle preventing our trip from measuring up to his idea of 'pleasure'. Likewise, Captain Jean's limited ability to respond didn't seem to make sense. He did regain his composure by punching the air, clenching his teeth, choking back a scathing and devastating response. But there was something else. When I deliberately dropped the toolbox, both Captain and seaman, as I mentioned, stopped dead. An argument as heated as the one I'd just witnessed isn't interrupted by such an insignificant incident, unless the clumsy person who caused it is the secret reason for the argument or, at the very least, is someone who they don't want to hear what's being discussed. The way the Captain raised his hand in greeting and his fake smile led me towards the second hypothesis. Captain Jean had clearly been putting on a show for me.

The manual work I was engaged in allowed me to reflect in relative peace and quiet. I spun the job out a little, carried on singing in a loud voice and decided to watch my step from now on. That was what I was going to do. I'd carry on ignoring Naguib and I'd show an unreserved admiration for Captain Jean, exactly as I had been doing up until a few hours earlier, as if no one had had an argument on the *Providence* or as if I myself hadn't heard anything apart from my own singing. Actually, had anything alarming really happened? The Cardiff-Glasgow dichotomy didn't throw any light on the subject of my hypothetical fears. But yes, something must have happened because to my surprise I found myself singing:

In taberna quando sumus
Non curamus quid sit humus
Sed ad ludum properamus

When we're down at the local tavern
We don't care that life is short
We just want to place our bets

I thought my voice sounded strange and tremulous.

The sudden appearance of Captain Jean stopped me from beginning the second verse. I think I went pale, but the Captain showed no sign of noticing that I was startled. He congratulated me on my work, lit the paraffin stove and poured himself a cup of coffee. For the sake of something to say (because I knew I should say something) I drew his attention to the pile of papers which, a few hours earlier, the wind had scattered across the floor.

'I haven't had time to sort them out,' I said.

'It doesn't matter,' he mumbled.

His warm-heartedness was still in evidence. I watched as he leaned over, holding his injured leg, and picked up a navigation chart.

'Careful,' I said suddenly. 'You're treading on the Pago-Pago girl.'

He looked at me in surprise. Then slowly he looked at the faded portrait that he'd just trodden on. After a moment or two's hesitation his face lit up, he let out what I thought was a sigh of relief and bent down again.

'Moriana,' he said. 'Moriana . . . this girl can never stay still!'

Then he burst out laughing and slipped the photo between the pages of a book.

I wanted to seem as chatty as usual, so I said, 'I see that we're using the engine today.'

'The wind's not in our favour,' he replied. But he didn't elaborate any further.

'I love the sea,' he'd confessed to me in Saint-Malo. 'I'll let you into all the secrets of sailing,' he'd promised. 'Us sailors, we're like a big family, you'll see,' But we were going full steam ahead, under engine power, to Glasgow, Captain Jean seemed to have lost any vestige of interest in teaching me anything and the beautiful Maliba, in just a few hours, had suddenly turned into Moriana. 'He's a serious conman,' I thought to myself. And I realized that the ferocious Malbú had never existed either.

5

For the next few days I obstinately carried on writing in my notebook, although I could no longer include the Captain's explanations, which were becoming few and far between, and my curiosity about all things maritime had notably diminished. However, I was careful not to note down my suspicions. As far as I was aware, Naguib couldn't read and Captain Jean couldn't speak a word of Spanish. But the strange atmosphere on board the *Providence* made it seem wise to act with the utmost caution. By now my travelling companions weren't even bothering to keep their conversations and arguments secret. I felt worse and worse and, convinced that I shouldn't let my feelings show, I decided not to become involved in their problems and to keep my distance, polishing pots and pans with the dedication of a true professional and not paying attention to anything that didn't directly concern me.

At the same time, as there were no more maritime lessons to write up, I threw myself into a letter-writing frenzy from which I couldn't expect any replies, not even an acknowledgement of receipt. I think that I ended up genuinely falling in love with Yasmine, and I told her so in one of the many letters I wrote to keep my mind occupied and to avoid facing up to the harsh reality of my situation. I was so sure that, once all this was over, I would be the first to be ashamed of such belated words of affection (and perhaps laugh at myself) and this kept my spirits up. The world did not end on board the *Providence*, and that voyage, which seemed to be lasting for ever, would have to come to an end eventually. Then I could look back on it as a brief parenthesis in my life or, better still (and I wanted to convince myself of this for all I was worth) as a simple manifestation of creative paranoia. However, once I ran out of things to write about and there was nothing left in the kitchen that needed to be washed or polished, my fleeting euphoria gave way to a disheartening feeling of dejection. There was no point trying to distract myself with fantasies or memories. Living in such close proximity with those two men was becoming unbearable, and it didn't seem unreasonable to imagine that, once they got bored with arguing with each other, they would end up taking their irritation and exhaustion out on me. The possibility that I could very quickly become a scapegoat for their differences of opinion (which remained a mystery to me) destroyed the last vestiges of my former aplomb.

No. I could no longer fool myself with passionate love letters or lose myself in ecstasy contemplating the ocean, which I had come to detest. Those two strange men didn't stop talking, telling each other to calm down and relax, discussing exorbitant sums of money as a cheque book with the logo 'National Bank' lay in the middle of the table and quickly became the absolute and indisputable focus of their attention. That had to be the reason for all their disagreements and arguments. I didn't pause to wonder whether I was in the presence of a pair of common smugglers or if, during the course of the voyage, the surly deck hand had discovered some sinister secret (in the Captain's past or in the depths of the hold) that had made him so outrageously greedy. I knew that Naguib was trying to sell his silence, to collect a share of who knew what dirty business and leave the Captain with no room for manoeuvre, while Jean himself became more and more worked up and unpredictable. But I also knew that, whatever the underlying reason, I needed to keep pretending to be unconcerned and indifferent. Naguib, to tell the truth, was making it difficult. Now he had just stood up and thrown out a question which could only have one answer.

'So, is everything clear?'

'When we get to Glasgow,' Captain Jean told him.

'No, Captain,' he said, and he seemed to place a slightly ironic emphasis on the word *Captain*. 'It has to be now.'

To my surprise, Captain Jean signed the cheque and handed it over to the Egyptian.

Out on deck there was the devil of a wind blowing and no

one, not even the most ardent enthusiast, could make a convincing case for going out for a breath of fresh air. I opted instead to remain seated at the table, lighting one of Naguib's cigarettes without bothering to ask his permission and waiting for someone, other than me, to decide to break the ominous silence that had fallen over the cabin like a lead balloon. A box of matches, that I was fidgeting with nervously, gave me an immediate excuse to withdraw out of view. I bent down and one by one, picked up all the matches which had fallen on the floor, and brushed the Captain's knee. I couldn't help noticing that the end of his scar, which was protruding from his trouser leg, had taken on a festering, purple hue. It looked both menacing and repulsive. Without thinking twice I stood up. That was when I felt Naguib staring at me fiercely. I desperately sought refuge in the Captain, but his glassy eyes only confirmed what, barely a few seconds earlier, I had just understood with an insulting clarity: that pair of crooks had done nothing less than share out a bounty. Their captive was standing there, like a fool, fidgeting with a box of matches, and was starting to experience, for the first time in his life, the true meaning of the word fear.

However, I couldn't say that the blood froze in my veins or that this was the only thing that happened to me for the extended time that I stood there motionless, faced with the cruel evidence. The sudden terror, which had paralysed my limbs, was immediately followed by the most dreadful intuition. Now I knew that I was a perfect idiot not only in the Captain's eyes but also, and more especially, in my own. Despite the fact that the wind was still howling with demonic fury, I went out on deck. Things had gone too far for me to be bothered about keeping up appearances. My head was spinning with everything that had happened and my mind was bursting with all sorts of childish plans which, this time, I was not about to consider. Now that Naguib had received his share of the loot and Captain Jean had realized that I was anxious, there would be no point to try and convince them of the sad reality. No. That the strange boy they had met one day in Saint-Malo, half arrogant and half innocent, was not a playboy millionaire. The refined education which he had sought to dazzle them with came from within the four walls of an old seminary, and he owed his patent disregard for the money that he had come into without any effort or merit, only to generosity or the vagaries of Fate. 'Too late,' I said to myself. And I pictured Grace selling properties, arguing with her agent again and vehemently cursing her only brother to whom, one fateful day, she'd had the unfortunate idea of gifting a year.

A fierce storm broke out during the night of 18th March that put the *Providence*'s obsolete rigging to a severe test. I welcomed it as a real blessing. I didn't know whether I was desperate or scared to reach dry land nor how long it would take for Captain Jean to beat the information he needed to demand my ransom out of me blow by blow. But the shipyards of Glasgow now turned out to be a much more urgent destination than the two of them had foreseen and, Captain and deck hand, committed body and soul to their task, both granted me once again the priceless favour of ignoring my presence. I resolved to listen carefully to the radio, not to become involved in their constant activity and to recover my serenity by furtively taking gulps of an aged rum which, in my folly, seemed to me to be the only friend left that I could trust.

At one point the Captain took off his bright red bomber jacket and put on a life-jacket. I copied him. Shortly afterwards Naguib did the same. But before he did so he carefully gathered up all his things (cigarettes, lighters and a few coins) in a headscarf and hung the bundle from a nail in the ceiling. He dropped it on the floor three times. I didn't bat an eyelid. I was too concerned with keeping my own balance to worry about anyone else but, even so, I couldn't help but notice the spectacular change that had come over my travelling companions. Naguib looked nervous and doom-laden. He followed Captain Jean's orders with a mixture of urgency and resentment, and his appearance had none of the arrogance and swagger of a few hours earlier. When the Captain ordered him to the prow to check the hatches were battened down, I breathed a sigh of relief. He was so anxious it threatened to become contagious.

Captain Jean, on the other hand, had regained the composure and authority he'd shown in the first few days of the voyage. He seemed to be comfortable in the face of adversity; the height of the waves and the wind's unusual strength seemed to make him increase in stature, as if he had been waiting for a crisis in order to show the pair of us what an old sea dog could do. Now, clutching the tiller, he poured out a commentary which I was in no condition to heed. 'Damn this storm!' he shouted, but I noted a glint of triumph in his eyes. And then, 'We'll ride out the storm as best we can and tomorrow, God willing, we'll make it to port.' And I nodded in agreement. My eyes red with alcohol, I nodded in agreement. Because I couldn't do anything else but nod my head, struggle intrepidly to stay on my feet and wait for the right moment to reward myself with another shot of happiness and optimism. Now I really could say, without any trace of irony, that the three of us were in the same boat. Glasgow emerged as the priority destination and I switched roles from being the silent protagonist of an ill-fated story into a discreet extra hand. And yet, Captain Jean was still putting on a act in front of me. It was as if he still needed my acquiescence, the naiveté which had led me to set foot on that old wreck and the aversion I'd felt to Naguib's rough demeanour from the word go. And yet, was there any trace left now of the deck hand's arrogance and brusqueness?

I would never find out. The Captain, who must have been very confident that luck was on his side (or, perhaps, he hadn't quite registered my lamentable state) suddenly ordered me to take over steering the ship. Such was my surprise that I didn't argue and I found myself grappling with the tiller in a super-human effort not to pass out. I didn't have time either to ask why he didn't wait for Naguib to arrive to take charge of such an important task or why he went out on deck with that strange expression fixed on his face. 'Just a few minutes,' he'd said. But the minutes stretched into a lifetime and, just when I had reached the limits of my endurance, when I was expecting one of the men to come and relieve me, the ever fainter voice on the radio was superseded by a desperate, agonising scream. At that moment I felt decidedly lucid and, half fatalistic, half resigned, I understood that the curtain had just come down on the farce.

A short while later Captain Jean appeared. He was panting like an old greyhound and his efforts to put on a pained expression seemed unnecessary and grotesque. When I gladly let him take over my place at the tiller, I avoided looking at his worried face. His very presence, now, made my stomach turn.

'It was a terrible accident,' he said.

But I wasn't interested in hearing the details. For example, how a loose boom had knocked the intrepid sailor overboard. Or perhaps the slippery deck was the culprit. Or maybe it was because the Egyptian was noticeably agitated. I went down into the cabin and stretched out on the bunk. I felt that the *Providence* lurching from side to side simply reflected my own anguish but, in spite of everything, stupidly, I started drinking again. This time to the health of the deceased man, to his boundless greed which had led him to overestimate his own strength, to the peace which he would now at last enjoy, for centuries to come, at the bottom of the ocean. My dreams were shattered by a violent shudder. When I stood up I saw the Captain's bomber jacket on the floor, and it seemed to be a brighter red than ever.

'Stop lazing around and get a move on,' I heard.

No, the Captain wasn't going to stand for extortionate claims and demands. I wasn't worth as much as the deck hand had made out and neither at any moment did Captain Jean have the least intention of letting go of a considerable amount of money which, possibly, he could never get back. But the storm, which had so conveniently facilitated a happy outcome to a criminal act, did not seem about to abate; quite the opposite. And suddenly, as I struggled to stay upright and a litany of curses and insults assailed my ears, I understood that, now that the deck hand had disappeared, my cooperation was turning into something valuable and indispensable. All that mattered for now was to guide the *Providence* safely into port. And the Captain needed me. It was something of a paradox, but he needed me in order to carry out my own kidnapping. Or perhaps I was nothing more than a useful witness to the storm, the flaws of the *Providence* and to Naguib's anxiety? A young man who, on reaching dry land, could be bamboozled again with incredible, fascinating stories. Making a huge effort, I climbed the steps which led to the bridge and looked at the Captain. I sensed he was annoyed, genuinely annoyed.

'Idiot!' he roared. 'Wake up!'

And then I tried to speak, to ask him why he suddenly looked so alarmed, to offer him all the help he needed. But my lips could only pronounce the word 'Moriana.' And, then, knowing that I was as drunk as a lord, I burst out laughing uproariously.

After that, everything happened very quickly. The Captain slapped me repeatedly around the face, told me to carry out his orders or face the most severe punishment. He said that we'd sprung a leak and needed to save our skins and said so many other things that they all became jumbled up and sounded like an irritating hum. But nothing could touch me now. Soon I hardly noticed him shaking me, his face began taking on Yasmine's features and his voice became sweet and melancholy. I knew that I needed to make a huge effort and stand up. But my friend, the rum, in which I had trusted so much, was exacting a high price. Now my head was spinning, I felt stabbing pains in my stomach and Captain Jean was no longer Captain Jean, or even Yasmine, but a host of deformed faces superimposed one on top of the other, with different expressions, coming towards me, unbelievably and monstrously large. I tried to convince myself that it was all just a nightmare and that I'd wake up. But I felt drowsy, so drowsy it was difficult to withstand. If I gave in to the drowsiness, if I let myself go, perhaps I could put a stop to that tiresome whirlpool of colours and I could believe I was back in the solitude of my cell. The first rays of sun slipping through the window bars, my precious books arranged in perfect order on top of the writing desk, the smell of coffee and toast; I knew that feeling so well. My body, still cold, warming up beside the fireplace in the library, strolling through the cloisters, conversations with fellow students, one day after another, the nocturnal birds flapping against the window pane. But I felt a painful pressure on my chest and my eyelids were as heavy as flagstones, my eyelashes stuck together. I had been ill, very ill. Someone was banging on the door to my cell and I had to open up. On the other side of the door, there were the principal, the

47

gardener and the brother doorkeeper. Yes, someone was banging on my door. They were going to knock it down, smash it in. And then, once again, the peace and calm of daily life.

But suddenly I felt my lungs filling up with water and I knew that I had to wake up or die. I opened my eyes and I had no option but to realize that I was not in the Seminary and I had not been struck down by fever.

That morning, I'm not sure of the date, I woke up for ever from an impassioned youth that had been both short-lived and wasted in equal measure.

Part II

6

Maybe because I'd always thought about death in the abstract, or as an alien or remote state, the discovery that I was still alive plunged me into the deepest and most terrifying despair.

I woke up enveloped in a pale light, freezing cold, covered in blood, soaked to the skin and with my hair encrusted with gravel and wet sand. I tried to remember the formula, the usual mechanism for my brain to issue an order and my knees to bend and force the rest of my body to stand up, breathe in the frozen air, restore the circulation to my veins and warmth to my lifeless hands. The impetus of a wave, smashing me into a rock, made my mind up for me. My only option was to grab hold of a rocky outcrop, draw on my depleted reserves and stand up.

I couldn't see more than a few metres because of the fog, but I was able to work out my immediate surroundings quite accurately. It wasn't a beach but a small cove where the outgoing tide, by the hand of Fate, had left enough room for me to live to tell this tale. I looked up at what I thought at first was a rock and I realized that I was at the foot of an impressive cliff. I couldn't quite see the top as the fog was so thick, but I could appreciate the pressing nature of my situation and the urgent need for action. I took a few steps along the bottom of the cliff, too tired to be concerned about my own condition. My legs were like jelly and my bloody chest showed through what was left of the life-jacket and there was sand everywhere: in my wounds, in the deep grazes on my arms, in the torn skin between my fingers. I stopped after a short while. I had just heard some dull, muffled noises, as if someone was banging on a door with brute force, or was working an old-fashioned fulling machine, or was desperately trying to call for help. The possibility of meeting up with my despicable travelling companions again, in such unforeseen circumstances, momentarily swept aside all my pent up hatred and made me run towards where the sound was coming from. I slipped on some loose stones as I was climbing over a boulder, but I managed to get up, finding some strength from God knows where and I came across the wreck of the *Providence*. I felt no emotion.

Part of the keel was embedded in a crack in the cliff-face, hanging at an angle because of the low tide and knocking against the walls of the cave, at ever-increasing intervals. There was no trace of the rest of the vessel. The part that remained seemed to have been cut off at such a clean angle that it looked as if it had always been like that, or it could have been a broken toy that a Cyclops had tired of playing with. I was overwhelmed by a sense of immensity. I wanted to shout, to scream for help, but either my voice refused to make a sound or my ears were unable to hear my own desperate cries. Then I realized that the boat crashing against the walls of the cave must, logically, have made a tremendous racket. I banged my fists on the *Providence*'s hull but all I could hear in response was the mocking sound of muffled clapping, dull and distant.

The situation was getting more and more distressing and allowed no room for doubts or self-pity. Seized by an unfamiliar instinct I scrambled on to the deck of the *Providence*. I don't know how many times I had to shuttle back and forth or how many times I was nearly put off by the creaking and groaning that was emanating from the hull. Neither can I remember even roughly how long it took me, armed with ropes and cables, to force open a chest or squeeze my way into the part of the cabin which had survived the shipwreck. I knew that time was working against me and that soon the waves would be crashing against the remains of the vessel again; that my salvation, in short, would depend on how quickly I could climb the cliff, protect myself from the cold and hold out, wounded and exhausted, until someone heard my cries for help. I discovered that the water had only partially destroyed the interior of what had been my cabin and that the Egyptian's things were intact, hanging from the ceiling in a bundle. I gathered up some blankets and tools and wrapped them in a sheet together with Naguib's bundle and tied it on my back. I was still hampered by the fog, but now I could clearly see the top of the cliff, its outcrops and crevices and, to my left, something resembling an old goat track which looked like the only possible way up.

The thought of a quiet village waiting for me at the top gave me enough courage to embark on the climb. The ropes and cables were a great help. I attached several of them to various outcrops, wrapped up my skinned hands with scraps from the life-jacket and began the ascent. Luckily it was not as high as I'd originally feared. The main difficulty lay in dodging the continual avalanches of loose rocks and defending myself from flocks of voracious seagulls, but I finally made it to the top, where I unloaded all the stuff and (to the extent allowed by the fog) surveyed the vast plain which opened up before my eyes.

But I didn't kiss the ground like they do in the old adventure stories and nor did I find enough motivation to jump for joy or fall on my knees and give thanks to the heavens for the miracle of my salvation. Laid out before me was the most desolate landscape I could ever have glimpsed in the worst possible nightmare. A vast expanse of gravelly sand, without a blade of grass, without a mere scrap of vegetation. A stony desert in which, however much I strained my eyes, I couldn't make out the outline of any building through the fog, or anything else to suggest that there might be a village nearby.

The unfamiliar instinct I mentioned earlier made me put aside any questions, place on hold any feelings of despair and spring into action again. I discovered that only a short distance away there was a small cave in the side of the cliff, big enough for me to shelter in. I put my things inside, undid the bundle, tied the scarf around my head and slid back down to the remains of the boat, using the ropes and cables. Many people might think I was rash to do this, but recent events and the strange energy which gripped me should be enough to convince them that I was acting as rationally as possible.

The idea of survival had taken hold in my mind. I didn't know exactly when my injuries and weakness would force me to stop, but I felt sure it wouldn't be long. I couldn't allow myself the luxury of collapsing in a heap. I tied one of the ropes around my waist, slid back down the cliff and, once aboard the *Providence*, I gathered up everything I thought I could carry. I strapped a new bundle on to my back, loaded with bottles of rum and gin, a couple of cans of food, a bag of sugar, some cotton wool and a few things which seemed essential at the time and which I later found no use for at all. Before I left the boat, by which time the hull was beginning to lurch with the rising tide, I put on the Captain's red bomber jacket over the remains of my shredded life-jacket. Back at the top of the cliff, I thought I heard for a second time the dull hammering sound of a fulling machine. But I didn't bother to look down.

The cave, which was very small, sufficed as a welcoming inn for a weary traveller. I covered the entrance with one of the blankets I'd brought up on my first ascent and spread the other over the uneven floor, sat down, switched on a torch and took stock of my possessions. After a few sips of gin I was able to look on the bright side. I was alive, I had a bit of food, a sheet I could use to bandage my wounds and alcohol to help them heal, Naguib's lighter and cigarettes, and Captain Jean's bomber jacket. I set light to some cotton wool soaked in rum, fixed the torch to flash intermittently and placed it outside the cave so that it could be seen from both land and sea. Then I went back into my shelter and, warmed up by the short-lived fire, I fell into a gentle sleep. 'Tomorrow,' I thought, 'it will all be over.' And, however incredible it might seem to me now, the truth is I fell into a deep sleep, as carefree as a baby.

7

But where on earth was I? The following morning, in the absence of any friendly or positive sign, I set out on a determined search for the Captain. The possibility that he might be sheltering in another cave, a short distance from the wreck, just as lost and shocked as I was, led me to waste precious time and to forget about my own sorry state for a whole day.

By the evening, however, my weariness and pain brought home to me the absurdity of my efforts. There was not a trace to be seen of Captain Jean, I was the only human being prowling around and about the *Providence*, and the most sensible thing would be to accept the fact, immediately, that I had been abandoned on a sinking boat and, from now on, I would have to rely exclusively on my own resources. I resolved there and then to consider the Cap-tain to be gone for good and to devote the next few days to looking after myself. I would make further trips to the boat, salvage the lighter pieces of timber and take away everything within reach.

I soon realized that no rescue would be forthcoming by sea. The torch started to get dimmer, the coastline was still wrapped in a thick fog and I couldn't ignore the fact that, even if some ship should happen to sail nearby, it would not do me much good, since I could scarcely hear a thing and my sore throat would not allow me to shout or scream in any case. My body, overcome by all its wounds, became a heavy burden to carry. But to my surprise, my brain was working at a furious pace. I wasn't bothered by the solitude: I had lived in perfect harmony with it for years. But I was alarmed at the speed I was going through my provisions, the refusal of my jellified legs to obey my instructions and my total ignorance of the place where Fate had deposited me. Occasionally, as I inspected the terrain without wandering too far from the cave, I reassured myself with comforting thoughts. I didn't know where I was, it was true. Scotland, maybe Ireland. But in Europe, in the second half of the twentieth century there were no longer any undiscovered lands, mysterious islands or any-where for a sort of anachronous "Adventures of Robinson Crusoe". People would come looking for me, I was certain, or alternatively, I would find them.

The constant humming in my ears was the worst of the afflictions I had to face. My sense of direction and balance had seriously deteriorated. My sense of smell, on the contrary, started to become unusually acute at around this time. I learned how to distinguish the smell of the rocks, the wind, and the mist which stubbornly settled over the land. I knew (although my hearing didn't help me at all) exactly how far away the flocks of seagulls were. Their proximity scared me and, when I sensed that they were too close, I took shelter in my cave. But, curiously, on my way back from my tentative daily expeditions, I was guided not by smells but, quite the opposite, by their absence. I had observed that all my belongings in the cave had no effect on my bloodhound-like nose, except to give it a moment's rest from its constant and exhausting labours. More than once, when darkness was already falling around me and the weak torchlight only served to confuse me, I closed my eyes and crept among the rocks like a stalking beast, and when I was forced to strain to discern any scent, then I knew that I was safe. My shelter, the remains of the previous night's fire and everything I had managed to rescue from the *Providence* would be just a few steps away.

Encouraged by this extraordinary faculty, I started gradually going on longer expeditions, taking great care never to leave without a bundle of provisions and a hip flask, in case my return was held up by bad weather. On one of these reconnaissance trips I discovered a spring. The water was muddy, with a high mineral content. It tasted strange and looked even worse. But I lapped it up with the exuberance of someone who has been rationing their provisions to the limits of tolerance, bathed my wounds and washed my hair, rinsing out the sandy clumps which I had started to think I would never get rid of. After completing my ablutions I felt reborn and reinvigorated and, I don't know why, I suddenly had an image of a Spartan warrior getting spruced up and dressing for battle. It was really stupid, but it was also a good omen. Because that day's expedition was crowned with success.

I noticed a hillock a short distance away. It can't have been more than ten metres high but its presence, in that desolate landscape, had the same effect on me as a huge mountain. I clambered up the side of it, choking back my emotions and once I reached the top I strained my eyes to see into the distance. At first I couldn't see anything worthy of mention: there were a few other mounds similar to the one I was standing on, without any signs of life or vegetation.

I sat down on a rock to catch my breath and reached for one of Naguib's cigarettes. I usually smoked a cigarette when my hopes of being rescued looked like being dashed, when the silence or the solitude became unbearable, when I was getting ready to go to sleep or after a tiring day of searching and failure. Until then I had never appreciated that just a pinch of shredded leaves could provide such companionship. So, I rationed my supplies, kept all the dog ends and, if I was in my shelter, I'd fall back on the old lag's trick of using a bottle to prolong the enjoyment of a cigarette after it's been put out. This time, however, I didn't get to savour the aroma and taste in the way I usually did, and nor do I remember taking the precaution of keeping the stub in my bundle. Up until then, blinded by the hope of a discovery, I had only looked out straight ahead, scanning the barren landscape with the patience of an explorer, trying to see through the wisps of fog and not allowing my imagination to be tricked into seeing what I wanted to see. But there was little to see there and, disappointed, I looked down instead at my immediate surroundings. I scanned the rips in my trousers, the cracked rubber of my boots, the pebbles which I had displaced scrambling up the mound, and suddenly my gaze fell on something that looked like a rudimentary hearth.

I slid down the side of the mound at full speed. Euphoria, that capricious emotion which would fill me to bursting one moment and abandon me the next, came flooding over me.

I was standing in front of a sort of sheepfold, some ten metres wide and five metres deep, equipped with an old hearth which was half in ruins, and a wooden board which could once have been part of a make-shift table. There was no door, although a couple of planks criss-crossing each other and swollen by the damp, indicated the place where there used to be one. The room was divided by a crude wall about a metre high: the larger half was completely empty; the smaller half had a chimney hood, the remnants of the table I mentioned earlier, a stewing pot and a couple of bronze bowls. The way that marvellous abode was positioned struck me as ideal. Inside, despite the absence of a proper door, I felt sheltered from the cold. The stone walls, blackened by the smoke of who could say how many fires, roast dinners and tanned hides, gave off a comforting warmth. Needless to say I immediately decided to convert that hut into my new encampment, but the reason for my overwhelming euphoria owed very little to the comforts offered by that unanticipated homestead. It had been abandoned a long time ago and the state of its sparse contents clearly indicated that no one had made use of this convenient shelter in recent years. However, the evidence that this building had once been occupied confirmed something that I had recently started to question too often. I had chosen the best, possibly the only, path.

I propped my bundle beside the hearth in a gesture which was full of significance for me and, after taking possession of the sheepfold, I retraced my steps, returning to the cave and reflecting on the least tiring way to move all my provisions and the most useful objects the following day. There were still a few hours left before it got dark and, convinced that good fortune comes in batches and that I was at the start of a favourable run of luck, I took the risk of slightly changing my route back. Survival. That was the only key to my salvation. Except that, from now on, I would have a refuge on a human scale, a warm cottage where I could recover my strength and calmly plan my next steps and devise strategies for someone to catch sight of me.

I felt so happy with the day's discoveries that I nearly didn't notice the third surprise Fate had in store for me. I had climbed up a fairly sizeable rock and, more out of habit than any real expectation, I looked out at the raging sea to the extent allowed by the cloudy conditions. I had never observed the coast from that vantage point and I was pleased to discover that, although visibility was still almost close to zero, there was a genuine beach, brim-full with pebbles, below me, just a short distance from my observation post. It was a bit late by then to go down and explore, and I made do with the reflection that the coast was not as inaccessible and cliff-bound as I had thought and that, in all probability, the sinister cliff face, which had so rudely welcomed my return to life, must have been a fluke, an unpleasant exception on a coastline which might hold real surprises for me. Even though I knew I was indulging in excess, I lit another of Naguib's cigarettes. But once again I wasn't about to savour its scented eastern aroma.

The pebble beach was divided into two halves by a wire fence, located halfway between where I was standing and the sea. Possibly, I had been looking at it without registering it. It didn't look like the work of an amateur. Although the first shadows of the evening prevented me

63

from imagining exactly what it was like, I could see its regular, implacable shape and some protuberances which I guessed, from a distance, must be metal barbs and other means of dissuasion. The day had been full of signs, clear evidence that I was getting close to something or someone but, much as I wanted not to, I couldn't help but admire the extraordinary presence of that fence in the middle of a landscape which, despite all my efforts, still hadn't revealed a single sign of life.

What was the fence meant to protect or guard? From my vantage point, the purpose of such a drastic measure could be none other than the sea. Raging waters, secret currents, whirlpools. It was not by chance that the *Providence* had been shipwrecked close by, nor that I was there now, weighing up the reasons behind my latest discovery. It seemed plausible. They had fenced off the sea to stop anyone wading into it from the beach and getting into trouble. But who would do that?

The wire fence confirmed the proximity of some settlement and the Authorities' concern for the welfare of its citizens, the expectation that someone might cross this desolate landscape and be faced, like me, with the treacherous, murderous sea. Unless it was the exact opposite. I felt a shudder and the question I had been putting off for so long resurfaced to torment me. Where was I, for God's sake? Where was I?

In taberna quando sumus
Non curamos quid sit humus...

But again, this time, despite the fact that my throat only issued forth a muffled sound, I suspected my voice was tremulous and scared. Because I found myself staring at the wire fence again and its barbed strands now seemed like the bars of an enormous cage in which I had been imprisoned.

8

I had to start writing things down. When your dreams start getting jumbled up with your memories, and tiredness and anxiety begin to take over, you need to use every trick in the book not to sink into the depths of despair. My situation was not so different from that of a condemned man, locked up in a dark dungeon, who doesn't know when he's going to get his next meal. I was scared of losing my sense of time. The nights were becoming clearer and clearer and the days darker and bleaker. The fog, an infernal curse determined to infiltrate every moment of my life, hampered my daily excursions, in which I placed so much faith. I had no points of reference apart from how quickly the firewood burned or the terrible weight of my own existence in those distressing circumstances. I decided to start writing things down and, when I did, I ignored the call of another voice imploring me to put the still pristine book to better (if ephemeral) use as fuel for the fire. But my needs went beyond eating and sleeping. In my new abode, I was protected from the cold, I had some provisions and the sea would hurl wounded fish, shellfish and great clumps of seaweed against the rocks, just as it had hurled me against those same rocks however long ago it was. The threat to my survival was not external: it came from within. That's why I had to persevere, there in my hut, with the stupid journal which I had so arrogantly started writing under the gaze of Captain Jean, and also with the passionate love letters which Yasmine would never actually receive. The only difference now was that I wasn't trying to overcome fear, I was dicing with madness.

One of the last things I had recovered from the shipwreck was a wooden chest with a rusty lock. I had been on the point of leaving it behind, not knowing what might be secreted inside and because of its awkward bulk. But, luckily, I hadn't given in to weakness and the idea that the chest might at least serve as firewood had outweighed my flagging reserves and fatigue. Now I congratulated myself on my foresight. Sitting by the warmth of the fire, I managed to unpick the lock. At first, I didn't find anything to bring me any cheer. Some old navigation logs, maritime charts of the Hawaiian Islands, of absolutely no use to me, and a notebook with blank, yellowing pages that might have been intended to record the details of a voyage which never actually took place. But there were also some rusty pens and several bottles of dried-up ink that didn't take long to be restored to its original state with a bit of heat and a few drops of water.

I was going to write everything down. I couldn't not do

it. The task of consigning the principal events of the day, my doubts and concerns to paper, loomed large as the only way for me to stay sane. And I had to start right then, before I was overcome with fatigue and relate how, barely a few hours earlier (if I could still presume to use conventional units of time), I had arrived at the cliff intending to fetch wood for the fire; how I had slid down the ropes and suddenly stopped in my tracks; how (to come to the point) the *Providence* had disappeared. I'm not saying that the waves had dashed the remains of the boat to pieces, striking a mortal blow and scattering its precious timber over the waters. I mean exactly what I said earlier: the *Providence* had disappeared. Because of the low tide you could still see traces of its presence at the entrance to the cave. But they were only traces. Someone had salvaged the boat with considerable skill and care. Who was this 'someone'? My bemused brain could only offer me unworkable hypotheses. Someone had spotted the remains of the vessel from a passing ship and had informed the authorities (although I still had no idea which country those authorities might belong to). But why would they be so bothered about cleaning up the shoreline when, as far as I could make out, I was the only inhabitant? Why hadn't they put some men ashore to see if there were any survivors? Why hadn't they climbed up the cliff, lit a bonfire, made tracks through the fog, armed with powerful search lights? The

Cyclops' broken toy had been thrown on to the high seas, far out of my reach, ripping away the last connection with my former world. Without the *Providence,* everything, even my own existence, was inevitably devoid of any meaning.

I dipped the pen in the watery ink, scratched at the paper and, by way of experiment, started writing mechanically, *'The Year of Grace'*. The unpremeditated irony of it didn't make me smile. My hand had already taken possession of the yellowing pages and slid across them driven by a powerful, feverish need. I read what I'd written back to myself, *'Although I spent the best years of my life with my back turned on the world . . .'* And I didn't stop writing until my hand was stayed by tiredness and the need to sleep.

Before wrapping myself up in the blankets I took a last look around me, as I usually did, with the help of the light from the weakly flickering flames. I was familiar with all my scant possessions down to the last detail, their exact location in the habitable part of the sheepfold, the shadows their outlines projected on the stone floor. It didn't take me long to notice a slight variation in what I had studied so many times and, as a special exception, I made use of the now feeble but precious light of the torch. There were all the ropes, the food, Naguib's scarf full of seaweed, the bowls, a pile of damp kindling drying out by the fireplace. I rubbed my eyes and confirmed that my visual memory had not deceived me. Because one of the two last bottles of gin had disappeared. Just like the *Providence*.

Once again, my thoughts turned to the Captain and the remote chance that he might be here on the island, hiding out in a hut similar to mine, fighting like me against the solitude and madness. But it was all too improbable. The Captain couldn't have done away with the remains of the boat, as if by magic. And I couldn't think of a good enough reason for him to avoid me or for him not to have needed all the many things I'd salvaged from the *Providence*. No, however desperate I might be for a companion in misfortune, I couldn't let myself be carried away by wishful thinking. Captain Jean was probably safe and sound, miles away from my refuge, certain in the knowledge that Naguib was lying at the bottom of the ocean. As for me, the only witness to his crime, blind drunk and abandoned to my fate, I wouldn't have taken long to join the impatient and hapless deck hand.

That night I dreamed about Maliba. She was in sunny Samoa, swaying gently in a hammock suspended between two gigantic palm trees, drinking coconut water and smiling at me. 'You're on your own,' she said. 'All on your own. All alone in a place with no name.'

9

Time, that incomprehensible presence that I felt unable to measure, became my closest ally. The tedious humming sound that had once assailed my ears had now become almost inaudible and my legs, fully recovered from cuts and bruises, had finally regained their natural agility, something that I needed now more than ever. On the other hand, my throat had shown no great improvement, stubbornly denying me the modest pleasure of talking to myself, greeting my small discoveries with yelps of triumph or cursing the misery of my confinement for all I was worth. But day followed night and night followed day and, by my calculations, it would soon be spring. Then, the fog would clear, the landscape would be bathed in sunlight and, perched on top of the low hills, I would be able to form a precise idea of where I was.

My more recent expeditions had not provided any concrete information to dispel my doubts. Wherever I looked (and my sense of direction had never been particularly good) I came across the sea. Gigantic waves breaking against walls of rock, or sand and pebble beaches protected by fine wire fencing. The prevailing bad weather meant that it was impossible to give a name to whatever I could see with any degree of certainty and, rather than a cohesive picture, all I had managed to form up until then was a series of disparate images, like a collection of postcards with no captions. I didn't reject the possibility that I was on an island, although it seemed more likely that I had simply been walking round in circles.

But I was not the only living being in that lost corner of the world. From time to time, I was gripped by a feeling (I'm not sure if it was welcome or not) that I was under close, invisible scrutiny, that the unexplained disappearance of the bottle of gin was just a small piece of evidence. My extraordinary sense of smell was now assisted by my hearing, and the tiresome fog which I hated so much was not the only thing the wind now brought to my front door. I was not alone. I could hear the bleating of goats or sheep, adding a significant piece of information to my random list of clues. If there were herds of animals, then there were also herdsmen, fields and pens. All I had to do was study where the wind was blowing from and follow the trail. A number of large rocks, which I had piled up like a pillar near my sheepfold in order to help me find my bearings on particularly gloomy days, gave me the evidence I was looking for sooner than I'd expected.

A sheep had got trapped among the stones of my make-shift monument and was desperately struggling to break free. Next to it, a young lamb was trying to catch hold of its mother's teats, without much success. The scene could not have been more tragic, but it didn't upset me. I had started grinding my teeth, my mouth was full of saliva and my tongue ran impatiently from one corner of my mouth to the other. I must have looked like a starving savage eyeing up his quarry. It seemed as if there was a strange light surrounding those animals, and for a moment it didn't register that their presence represented a guarantee that I would be rescued.

I approached them cautiously, rope in hand. I had never seen such a strange breed of sheep. Their rough fleece grew in clumps, leaving large bare patches of grey skin all over their bodies from head to tail. They appeared to be covered in pustules and scabs and gave off a terrible stench which was so strong that, in spite of my carnivorous needs, I nearly abandoned the task. However, it wasn't me who decided. My instincts took over without consulting me. After managing, with admirable skill, to pin them both down and calming down the furious wounded mother, I convinced them, by beating them with the rope and pelting them with small rocks, that they were now under my power and that they had no option but to be led quietly to my hut.

I wasn't quite so proficient when it came to trying to milk the mother. The animal's stubborn refusal to share her milk and her loud bleating as she fought off my attempts, put paid to my last shred of sanity. In no time at all I'd changed from a poor castaway into a cruel and voracious savage, and God only knows what I could have been capable of in that situation or any other that Fate might have decreed for me. I killed one of the sheep by beating it with the wooden chest and with the rocks and ropes, but instead of sating my anger on the mother I chose the little lamb which, terrified, scarcely put up any resistance. That's what I did and the reason for my choice was not so much the exquisite quality and delicacy of fresh young lamb meat, but rather an overwhelming desire to teach the noisy, stinking, wounded mother a lesson. She was going to stay with me in the fold, give me her milk whenever I wanted and, guided by hunger and instinct, lead me to the pastures where she'd left her sisters and to the cabin where her owner lived. I skinned the lamb in a mad fury, threw its head in its mother's face, drank its blood with passionate delight while it was still warm and, with more haste than expertise, I chopped up one of its legs and roasted the pieces on a skewer over the fire.

A simple flame was all that was needed to fill the shelter with the long-forgotten aroma of barbequed meat. I didn't have the patience to wait and before long I sank my teeth into the first piece. The sheep's bleating no longer annoyed me. Driven by cruelty or madness I wanted to show my prisoner how quickly the fruit of its womb was going to disappear into my mouth and I turned to face her. The sheep ignored me. It was still tied up to the boards which served as a door, but it had stopped struggling to get free. It seemed to be concentrating on something outside, indifferent to my barbarous feast. It didn't make a sound or move a muscle. And yet, I could make out the unmistakeable bleating of a sheep or two, or maybe a whole flock. I rushed outside the hut and climbed the hill. Then I saw them. I swear to God I had to sit down to stop myself slipping over and I pinched my nose so as not to faint.

They were sheep, no doubt about it. Twenty, thirty, maybe fifty sheep. They looked similar to my prisoner, only now, seeing the whole flock, I didn't know what to make of the fact that they all had the same pustules, the strange fleece, similar wounds and looked just as ferocious. They were standing at the bottom of the mound, arrayed in a strange formation as if ready for battle, which the ensuing events quickly proved to be the case. Two rams with impressive horns were bleating noisily. They sounded more like wild beasts than ordinary, inoffensive ruminants. They were in the centre of the group and were clearly poised for confrontation. It seemed to me that the fight would boil down to making a lot of noise or to a show of strength in front of the opponent. But what I was witnessing was just the warm up. After a short while, the rams began to lunge at one another, performing arrogant pirouettes, balancing on their hind legs, seeking out each other's weak spots with such desperation that, suddenly alarmed, I decided to go to ground and hide among the rocks and the moss.

It wasn't a game or some kind of rite or ceremony. The flock of sheep, following the fight blow by blow, struck me as even more terrifying than the antics of the combatants. But, to my momentary relief, the duel was short and, when one of the rams rolled over on the ground, defeated, the pestilent sheep instantly stopped bleating. However, the silence would last no more than a few minutes.

I was just about to stand up when the sheep, which until then had only been restless spectators, started to jostle each other, letting out terrifying screeches and rolling around among the rocks. It was as if they were seized by an irrepressible state of agitation. The bravest ones managed to beat a path through the foul-smelling flock and approach the wounded ram. I never would have thought that a sheep's hooves were capable of ripping away the hide of a dying beast, tearing out its eyes or stripping out its entrails in short order, maybe because I'd never, until that day, had the occasion to observe such hooves or that kind of sheep. I looked on as the flesh was scorned in favour of the viscera, which were fought over with the most absolute ferocity. When one of the sheep managed to secure a portion of lungs, heart, liver or intestines, it withdrew a few metres from the group and, with great skill, dissected, pulverized and blandished its bloody trophy.

I couldn't make head or tail of the macabre banquet that I'd just witnessed, but at the time I had other more immediate concerns, which filled me with dread. One of those feral beasts was waiting for me at the door to my shelter, and who could say whether by now it had freed itself from the thick rope that I'd managed to tie it up with: furious, humiliated, ready to feast on me in the same way as its sisters were banqueting on the remains of the ram.

I returned to the sheepfold with my heart in my mouth, desperately trying to convince myself that the sheep was too badly wounded to do battle with me, that it might have died or that, free of its bonds and feeling unwell, it had opted to run away from my sadistic madness. When I arrived at the door, I stopped. The sheep was still there, twisting around on the ropes that were now tinged with blood, beating its head against the boards of the door, desperate not to miss the party, from which the sound of sinister bleating could still be heard. My senses were dulled by the feeling of being in the presence of a monster. Fear turned into anger, dejection into savagery. I executed my prisoner with the cruelty of a desperate man. I stoned it, kicked it, stabbed it, until my own fury turned on myself and, spurting blood, I banged my head against the walls of the shelter. I had seen the hooves, long sharp knives capable of chopping up a ram as skilfully as any butcher.

77

But what had I actually seen? Could I have been hallucinating? Could it have been a cruel illusion produced by fatigue, desperation and hunger?

I was too tired to play the dual roles of victim and executioner. I collapsed on top of the blankets, wrapped Naguib's scarf around my head and laid there, delirious with fever, for hours, days or weeks. Until I felt a rough, wrinkled hand settle on my forehead.

Part III

10

I apologize, hypothetical reader, for the frequent changes in mood that have punctuated this story of my travels. Back in those dark days I was writing for myself, to hoodwink the phantom of madness, to forget that all it needed was one moment of resolve and my nightmares and, in particular, I myself, would pass happily into a better life. Fortunately, I didn't succumb to the temptation, although I have to admit that on one occasion I was on the point of jumping off the top of the cliff and, another time, I tried to burn myself to death in the flames of the small fire in my shelter. I lacked the courage for the former and the determination for the latter. To this day, as well as the memories, I still have grazes from the first incident and a scorched trouser leg from the other. On both occasions (and on so many others when desperation hovered on the threshold of my consciousness) an extraordinary faith, that would embarrass a less sensitive person, came to my rescue at the last moment. It wasn't an erudite faith, the sort which could have sprung from the long period of time I spent in the seminary; it was something more akin to a pact between a mortal and the Divinity, like the relationship that a bereaved old lady might have with a superior and omnipotent Being who can be seduced, persuaded, haggled with or, in the last instance, angrily denied the trust that had been confided in it.

During that period, I pledged to undertake some hare-brained schemes. Once I had been rescued and had gone back to the world I'd been excluded from, I would lock myself away in the seminary again and scourge myself every night until I bled, and I would walk barefoot to remote shrines, with chains on my ankles and nothing but a flask of water and some dried bread to last me the whole journey. Frequently, my pledge didn't seem to sufficiently match the favour that I hoped to obtain, and I'd insert some modifications. I'd do without the scrap of bread and the flask of water, add a chain around my waist and impose an absolute rule of silence on my walks and (another innovation) these would now take place only at night and in the coldest winter months. As the days went by, all identical, and my feverish mind was gripped again by depression, I discarded the latest pledge and thought up another one, down to the last detail, until I was convinced that this was the definitive version, that the Great Beyond (which had never seemed so tangible and at the same time so abstract) would have no choice but to accept the pact. I never questioned whether my new vows were really any better than the old ones, whether they cancelled out the previous ones or whether, on the contrary, I was accumulating a long list of sacrifices and forfeits. But now, as my mind is making progress towards achieving a definitive state of calm, I look back on some of those pledges (in particular the one about observing a strict fast for forty days alone in the Gobi desert) as even less appealing than the situation I was trying to escape, and I have to smile at the lack of imagination brought about by my anguish. But anyway, I shall try not to got get lost in idle ramblings, and keep to the main storyline.

After my first encounter with the diseased sheep and their sinister rituals, I remained in a feverish stupor, very nearly delirious. I didn't know whether I was awake or dreaming. When I closed my eyes I kept seeing the gory banquet I had just witnessed. When I opened them, the stench of my own living space transported me once again into that incomprehensible nightmare. I didn't know which was better, my dream world or reality, and I couldn't tell for certain if, at that point, I was actually in my shelter or, on the contrary, still out in the open, lying on the ground with my head buried in my hands.

At one point (I'm not sure whether I had my eyes open or closed) I thought the dead sheep had come back to life and that I wasn't alone in the sheepfold. Another time, I felt something like the touch of a cold hand resting on my forehead. Things immediately became more complicated. I was a ram and my voice was deep and rough. Obviously, I was the ram that had lost. I was so acutely distressed that this time I did manage to wake up. In the darkness, I could make out the shape of someone rummaging through my things and I remember sitting up in bed, unable to make any sound except for a sort of shriek. Or was that afterwards? The shape came towards me and I realized that I was experiencing a terrifying hallucination. It was a man, an extremely filthy man in rags. He looked at me with a strange expression, fixing his eyes on mine with dilated pupils.

It was a man. His body was like a man's in every respect, but there was something in his face that was reminiscent of those monstruous feral sheep from which there was no escape, even in my dreams. I'm almost certain that I passed out, once or several times, because I remember in flashes that the strange creature gave me something to drink and said something that, at first, I didn't understand, and then he covered me with a stinking, reeking sheepskin which made my senses cloud over.

Then, for the first time for so long, I began to speak. A torrent of possibly meaningless words which he then repeated to himself in a husky voice and which he seemed to understand. When I had the strength to stand up a few days later, I discovered that I hadn't been dreaming, that my strange nurse was called Grock and that he and I were the only human beings on the island. That morning my life took a complete about turn.

We were on an island, according to my calculations somewhere in the Hebrides, just a few miles off the Scottish coast. So I wasn't at the edge of the world, as I had begun to fear, but quite the opposite, and this was the fact (that I was so close to civilisation) which shocked me to the core. I had been on the verge of becoming a savage, and what previously might have seemed dramatic now struck me as a perverse trick of Fate. Hadn't I gone looking for adventure? Hadn't I instinctively felt, in those far-off days in Saint-Malo, that the time for action had arrived, that the hundreds of books which had given me so much pleasure as a child were suddenly about to turn into fragments of my own life?

The certain knowledge that, once the fog had dissipated, I would be able to see the Scottish coast as clear as day filled me with joy and, at the same time, made me feel completely ridiculous. I consoled myself with the thought that, had it not been for Grock's miraculous appearance, I would not be in a fit state to analyse this or any other feeling, however embarrassing it might seem now.

The old man had become the strangest and most attentive of nurses, and I'm not unaware that his motives were not entirely unselfish, and that his self-appointed task of restoring me to life was only tangentially related to what is known as a humanitarian act. But that was at first, long before Grock and I became friends, if it's possible for a crofter like Grock and a castaway like me ever to become friends.

How can I begin to describe my saviour in a few words without tainting them with gratitude? In the eyes of the world, Grock was probably just a coarse, simple crofter whose enforced isolation, together with life's deprivations, had led to his behaviour regressing and his physical features degenerating. But what's certain is that, out of all the images that reality and delirium had to offer me, seeing Grock was, without any doubt, one of the most pleasant, despite the fact that his face had similar pustules to those of the bloodthirsty sheep, his voice sounded almost inhuman and his movements were strange and clumsy, as if he were struggling with a secret inclination to relinquish his upright stance but didn't dare to get down on all fours to wander across his arid, rocky domains.

Perhaps I'm exaggerating a little and the similarity he bore to the ruminants, which I noticed right from the start, was only due to the unusual effects of their prolonged coexistence. Because when, a few days later, I was able to see the incredible ease with which Grock climbed up or down the cliff, ran up hills or popped up here and there through the fog without doing himself the slightest injury, I had to admire him and I realized that I was the one who was really out of place and grotesque in that inhospitable environment, and that what had previously seemed monstrous now seemed like the most natural thing in the world. Similarly, the sheep (which, of course, I tried to avoid) no longer made such an impression on me. Those savage creatures were afraid of Grock. They would leave a field at his command and, albeit resentfully, they would allow their master to milk them, not out of obedience, I assumed, so much as fearing God knows what punishment Grock was capable of inflicting upon them. So I stopped feeling scared of them (at least not as much as when I first came across them) and I even got used to the stench which heralded their proximity. The task of milking them was reluctantly undertaken by the crofter, whose own charming aroma was not exactly a delight to the senses. But, as I said earlier, I'll try not to digress.

The first word the old crofter spluttered over my sick bed (as far as I can recall) was 'Grock'. At the time, confused by the illusion that the creature in front of me was half man, half sheep, it didn't occur to me that my timely visitor was even capable of uttering his own name, and I took it for a bleat. But my long convalescence and the strange lucidity which is often the result of fever doubtless led me to stammer out various phrases in different languages until I realized that Grock was speaking in a rudimentary English, peppered with expressions in Gaelic (a language that, unfortunately, I had no knowledge of at all, except for the fact that it existed). I also realized that if I left out any kind of fancy words and kept, instead, to the most basic forms, my saviour's eyes lit up and he either nodded or shook his head and tried, for his part, to keep his language simple and restrict himself to naming things.

Consequently, learning Grock's language was not too difficult and I was helped not so much by my excellent knowledge of English as by the fact that his peculiar syntax was very similar to that of certain primitive languages and, even, to the language used by small children who have a limited range of vocabulary when they first start expressing their needs. Grock's sentences would often start directly with the material object of interest, then went on to the secondary issues of how and why and in what circumstances, and only afterwards, a long time afterwards, to the actual reply to my questions. I asked him repeatedly about the name of the island, and he would always reply, 'Grock.' I tried to be more specific and, along with gestures and facial expressions, I said, 'Island. This island. What is it called?' The answer was invariably, 'Grock.' He obviously made no distinction between his own name and the name of his property. Grock had spent too many years in the company of sheep.

But I couldn't grumble about my luck. Thanks to the care extended by the crofter and the information I managed to drag out of him, with consummate patience, I was able to form an approximate idea of the place where we were located. In earlier times Grock's island had been inhabited by several families of crofters. Afterwards, ('long, long time ago'), for reasons the old man didn't know or couldn't explain, the families collected up their things, abandoned their flocks and left the island. Only Grock had stayed, in charge of hundreds of sheep, the mothers of the mothers of the mothers of the quadrupeds which had made such an impression on me. Whether it was because there were too many of them for one man to control or because he just neglected them, as far as I could make out it didn't take long for them to become unruly and for the passive flocks to turn into bloodthirsty marauders.

'They did bad things to Grock,' he said. 'Very bad things.' I soon noticed that the crofter hated them with a vengeance. When he spoke about the sheep his face took on a terrifying aspect, his eyes shone with a savage fury and he delighted in reciting the long list of punishments he'd subjected them to, in order to show them that he was Grock, master of the island, and that they had done 'very bad things.' When I eventually asked him what the bad things they'd done were (secretly fearing that he'd tell me) his eyes lit up again with a ferocious glow which dilated his pupils. Then, unexpectedly, his expression became sad and he replied, 'They killed Grock.'

During the first few days we spent together I often had to use my imagination, and sometimes pure invention, to interpret his disconcerting revelations. He was convinced that I came from Glasgow (although perhaps that's what he called everything unrelated to the island) and appeared to be very surprised by the story of the shipwreck, my survival and the subsequent disappearance of the remains of the *Providence*. I don't think that Grock, who was as spontaneous as a child, was capable of lying, and I was astonished by the absurd possibility that the old man knew nothing about the boat's mysterious disappearance. Once again, I considered the number of enigmas that remained unresolved and I suspected that the sketchy narrative skills of my saviour were not going to be of much use to me, for the moment.

I was absorbed in these dark conjectures when Grock, who had just consumed a hefty portion of my last bottle of gin, burst out laughing like a wild man. I didn't have any time to be surprised. As if suddenly remembering why he was so excessively happy the old man tore off a locket which was hanging around his neck opened it and took out a crumpled bit of card which he handed to me, still laughing. Now I really did need to rub my eyes to convince myself that I wasn't dreaming. I was holding a colour photograph, a picture of the crofter himself, taken with a Polaroid camera. So the island was not quite as abandoned as I had been given to understand. I didn't stop to think about who could be disturbed enough to come up with the macabre idea of taking Grock's photograph, nor did I think it was the right time to interrogate the crofter on the matter. All I could do was join in his laughter to show my good intentions. He, in turn, between fits of laughter, told me about the small box on which you pressed a button and there would slowly appear shadows, then some colours, then finally the image of a man. 'A man,' he said. The apparent magic of the camera was what really amused the crofter.

I looked at the polaroid photo again with a shudder. What I held in my hands was a cold, crude representation of horror. And I realised that the creature that was writhing about in front of me was scarcely more than a child, a mad old child who, I was absolutely certain, had no idea that he was laughing at himself.

11

When I was strong enough to stand up and walk under my own steam, Grock told me to accompany him. I didn't put up any resistance. On the contrary, I pretended not to have noticed his harsh tone, which didn't invite any argument, as fresh proof of my intention to bow to his authority and respect his territory. It was early morning and we walked for a good while, assisted by a feeble daylight in which the old man seemed to move with total ease. Grock didn't say a word as we went along and, grateful to have a break from the wearisome task of interpreting, I spent my time taking note of the scant features of that desert-like landscape, still suspecting that, if I tried to come back along the same route on my own, I wouldn't be able to find my way. I had never explored these paths, as a result of my decision not to stray too far from the coast, and I was so weak that more than once I was tempted to close my eyes and fall to the ground. When I was about to reach the limits of my strength, the crofter pointed towards some shadows and we both increased our pace.

I was pleasantly relieved when I saw Grock's home. It was a rudimentary abode, with just the bare essentials: a fire-place, a table, a couple of chairs and a bed. But to my castaway's eyes that simple furniture seemed the height of luxury, a thing to be envied. There was a shelf along one wall with several cheeses in various stages of maturing. My host grabbed one of them and swallowed it in one mouthful. I realized that poor Grock was just as hungry as I was and, without waiting to be invited I also took a portion of that long-forgotten delicacy. I can't comment on the quality of the cheese or the crofter's skill at cheese making. The provenance of the milk was obvious but even that didn't put me off. I gobbled down the cheese and immediately felt full and sat down, slightly euphoric, on one of the rustic chairs which unexpectedly made me feel like a human being again.

Grock was poking the ashes of the fire and seemed to have forgotten about me altogether. I took the opportunity to have a look around. There were a number of empty bottles lying on the floor and some sheepskins hanging from the ceiling. Without getting up, I leaned over towards the only window in the room. Outside I could see a small mound topped with a cross, and I was pleased to note that, despite his isolation, the old savage respected the dead and still had some religious sentiments. Comforted by these discoveries, I stood up and went towards the corner, where there was a large pile of bottles. I immediately recognized one of them as the bottle of gin that had gone missing. I smiled tenderly at the thought of my thief-benefactor and looked at the others. There were whisky and brandy bottles or, to be precise, there were receptacles which had once contained whisky and brandy. The labels were not too worn: some even looked as if they'd just left the shop. Once more I was encouraged by the thought that we were not as isolated as I'd feared. I picked up one of the bottles and showed it to Grock. Almost instantly I realized that I shouldn't have. The crofter looked at the bottle with a fierce desire, his eyes glinting like a wild animal, then he looked me up and down and, finally, rested his gaze on my startled face, as if he had only just recognized me or, much more likely, had suddenly remembered what had been keeping him awake at night. 'Bottles,' he bleated. 'Give Grock bottles. Now!'

My incomprehension only made him angrier. He grabbed me by the neck, shook me and hurled me violently on to the bed. As I fell, I knocked my head on a shelf and nearly lost consciousness. Grock, standing right next to me, gave me no respite. He uttered a few unintelligible grunts and then, with stunning clarity, he blurted out, 'Bottles! Find more bottles!' Then he threw me against the wall again.

So that was it. The old drunkard had dragged me back from death's door so that he could discover what he suspected was a secret store of alcohol. Right then I couldn't have wished for anything more than a stash of gin to slake his mad thirst! I'd have to escape, there was nothing else for it. I'd lie to him and come up with a plan as quickly as possible to buy some time. Grock was kind enough to release my neck and confined himself to staring at me fiercely. I looked at one of the bottles. If I managed to jump up and grab it I could, at least for a short while, keep the crofter at bay. Then I would promise him anything that came into my head, I'd promise him anything he wanted until he calmed down and I could decide on the right time to smash the bottle over his head. 'Calm down,' I said. 'Let's all calm down a bit.'

When I stood up I realized that my head hurt like hell and that however much I tried I wouldn't be able to execute that amazing pirouette which had so inspired my imagination. 'The bottles–' I began, but then suddenly broke off. I could see the cross again through the window and I remembered Grock's photograph and how pristine most of the whisky labels were. The fate which the crofter had in store for me couldn't have been more obvious. But instead of being shocked I was furious. With a strength I didn't know I possessed, I jumped on the old man without giving him a chance to be surprised. I'd lost control and I fired off questions without waiting for answers. All I wanted was for that murderous savage to confirm my suspicions so that I could do away with him. 'The photo!' I shouted. 'Who took your photo?'

Grock looked at me with the sudden innocence of a child. Then I grabbed the locket and showed him the photograph.

'The box,' I said. 'Whose was it? Who made "a man" with that box?'

'Men!' he spluttered, after a pause.

'Men?' I repeated, and I was careful not to let go of his neck. 'What men? Where are the men?'

The crofter took an age to respond.

'Glasgow,' he replied, finally. 'Men from Glasgow. Come to see Grock.'

'OK,' I shouted, without understanding much of what I was hearing. 'And so, what did you do with the men? Did you kill them with your axe and bury them outside your front door? Did you pray for their souls and make a cross for them? Is that what you were going to do with me?'

I realized that I had increased the pressure on Grock's neck so much that he couldn't speak even if he wanted to. When I let him go he seemed more surprised than angry.

'Men,' he said. 'Men from Glasgow. Come to see Grock. Bring him bottles. Go back to Glasgow. Find more bottles for Grock.'

'In that case,' I asked, now completely lost, 'who is out there, under the cross, next to the front door?'

'Grock,' he said. And he burst into tears.

My strange host's frequent mood swings, as well as his irritating ability to lose the thread of our conversations, led me to watch out for the smallest sign that the former was about to occur and to take full advantage of the opportunities created for me by the latter. The truth is that it was not at all easy. Forewarned by my recent experience, when he furrowed his wrinkled brow unexpectedly I lost no time in trying to guess the reason behind his burgeoning anger. I would say the first word that came into my head, point something out which had nothing in the least to do with what we'd been discussing and even, on some occasions when the expression on his face made me fear for my own safety, I would start to leap and prance about, bursting into song, making gestures, pulling faces, nodding and bowing, which had the miraculous effect of entrancing Grock momentarily and dispelling his dark thoughts. I soon became an expert in the art of interpreting my unpredictable Man Friday and, even though I couldn't understand everything he tried to explain to me, in answer to my questions, I did at least manage to gather some information of the utmost importance for the future.

They, the 'men from Glasgow', came to the island on a regular basis. They arrived in a launch, inspected Grock's dominions and left again by nightfall, never forgetting to leave several cases full of bottles on the sandy beach. I didn't quite manage to discover in what capacity the visitors came. Were they the island's real owners or a simple reconnaissance patrol? The crofter would receive these welcome guests every other year, which would have been disheartening for me had Grock not pointed to the empty bottles and added, with absolute certainty, 'Soon. Back soon.' His conviction was enough for me to believe every word he said.

Likewise, the cross that I had first glimpsed through the window no longer gave me the slightest cause for concern. Whoever lay buried there, a couple of metres or so from the front door of the cabin, was the living being the crofter had most loved in the world. He told me so several times, through a mixture of tears and anger, with a clarity rarely found in his syncopated monologues, as if his memory had become stuck at that point in time and, from then on, his life had been locked in a prison of shadows. 'Long time ago,' he would say, and Grock always told the story using the same words, possibly having repeated it time and again to the wilderness or tirelessly committing it to memory. 'They did lots of things. Bad things to Grock.' A long time ago, in the years after the families had left the island and Grock had refused to abandon what he considered to be his. Those were happy years. Nobody told Grock what to do, and he and his sheepdog came and went freely across their territory. Never in the world had there been a creature as intelligent as his companion. He had taught him how to round up the sheep and, at nightfall, when he heard the dog's barking, he knew that the flocks were returning in an orderly fashion and he went out to meet them. But one evening the crofter didn't hear his dog barking and not one sheep came back to the fold. He was very surprised and walked out to the fields with a strange fear in his heart. He didn't find the sheep, and nor did his friend respond to his calls. He had to wait until the first light of dawn to realize with horror what had just happened. His dog was lying on the grass with his belly ripped open, pouring blood. His eyes had been torn out and the rest of his body was covered in hoof marks, as if the whole flock had rounded off their criminal act with a posthumous act of mockery. Mad with rage, Grock armed himself with sticks and rocks and set off in pursuit of the rebellious sheep. The first ones to cross his path perished within a few minutes of their encounter. The second batch were granted the privilege of a prolonged agony, dragging themselves along, mortally wounded, for hours on end, until not one drop of blood remained in their revolting bodies. He spared the lives of the third batch. But first he took care to beat them black and blue so that they understood the gravity of their punishment. After a couple of days, exhausted by this gory activity, he gathered up the remains of his dog and buried them at the entrance to his house. And there lay Grock, or, in his own words, the creature which Grock had most loved in all the world.

The crofter's tears were even more unbearable than his fits of rage.

12

I stayed in Grock's home for about a week. I'm still not sure
if it was voluntary or because that was what my host had
decided. But what was certain was that, in addition to the
usual bad weather on the island we now had, first a hail
storm, then a thicker fog than normal, which reminded me
of how cold my shelter was and the harshness of my daily
struggle to survive. In contrast, in the cabin we enjoyed a
few home comforts: a fireplace to warm us up, a decent
stock of firewood and enough food to sate the hunger of a
dozen men like Grock and me. During the day, he taught
me (or rather, forced me to learn) how to make cheese and
curds using the most primitive methods. I paid close
attention, although I was well aware that, if I ended up on
my own, it would take an enormous effort for me to be able
to milk any of those sheep. At night, the old man would lie
down on his bed and I would do the same on a pile of
sheepskins that I'd placed on the floor. I don't remember
sleeping very well any of those nights. The crofter snored
so violently and, forced by circumstances to be cautious,
despite being dead tired, I didn't dare to try any of the
usual remedies: whistling or clicking my tongue, for fear

that if he woke up suddenly my forgetful rescuer might not remember why I was there. But that was not the worst of it.

As soon as I'd finished my daily chores as an impromptu cheese maker, the old man draped a couple of sacks over my shoulder and ordered me to follow him. It was no use complaining about the bad weather. Grock seemed to have made up his mind to make the most of my company and to assign me task after task, even though he didn't really need anything apart from the pleasure of being obeyed. I followed him at a distance, resentfully. That simple old man was nothing like the faithful Man Friday out of the only novel that, ironically, I had forgotten all about when I saw the *Providence* that day in Saint-Malo, which now seemed a very long time ago. Quite the opposite. At times, Grock took on the features of the wicked old man with hairy legs in one of Sinbad's most terrifying stories and I, just like the humiliated sailor, would sooner or later have to come up with some kind of ruse to extricate myself from his growing tyranny. However, I knew I had to be clever about it. If I represented nothing more than a whim for Grock, he, in contrast, was the only chance of salvation I had found since I arrived on the island. I was engrossed in these thoughts when I realized that we were heading towards my shelter and I felt a strong yearning to be on my own again. But the crofter had other plans that from my point of view were not quite so auspicious. When we reached the crossroads, the old man took the opposite path and I had no option but to follow him. The wind had dispersed the thick fog and, for the first time in a long while, I could see the path clearly. That's how I discovered to my delight that we were heading towards a dense forest. I took off the sacks and, ignoring Grock's shouts, I began to run like a madman.

It was a forest, the first significant sign of vegetation I had seen on the island. But, as I approached it, I was struck by its strange shapes, the intricate thicket of trunks and roots, the darkness that you could see beyond the first line of trees where I now stopped to catch my breath, overheated and panting. Was it the running that had tired me out? I carried on for a few metres and leaned against one of the trunks. Then I realized that the way I was standing was the same as most of the trees, which were leaning in against one another, intertwined, falling in on each other, as if they were all part of one single, sinister being. I didn't have time to dwell on this gloomy impression. The trunk I was leaning against suddenly collapsed under my weight, falling to the ground without making a sound, followed by other nearby trunks. Suddenly the forest had started moving. 'It's dead,' I shouted. 'It's a dead forest.' And I ran back out.

Grock was standing a few metres away with a look of panic in his eyes. He was carrying the two sacks that I had jettisoned in my mad dash and was looking at me now as if I were an apparition, back from the dead, someone he hadn't expected to see again after a voyage into the region of shadows. When I approached him, the old man was shaking like a leaf. He didn't say a word but, from his fixed stare at the forest, I thought I understood that Grock would never have dared cross the first line of trees. I couldn't mock him for being stupid or irrational because I myself had just succumbed to a stupid and irrational fear. I went a bit closer and, with the best intentions, I patted him on the back. For an instant the old man gave me a tender, scared look. Just for an instant. Then he quickly went back to normal and pointed enthusiastically towards a hollow that, in the heat of the moment, I hadn't noticed. That was where we had been heading, and nowhere else. The hollow was full of tree trunks and timber that Grock, unhooking an axe from his belt, exhorted me to chop up, place in the sacks and carry on my back.

'Back soon,' he'd said. 'Men from Glasgow. Back soon.' I forgot about our brief moment of communication in the grip of fear and remembered that he had plenty of firewood stored at home and, at that moment, I no longer had the slightest doubt that the old man had decided to make me his slave.

13

When I got back to the cabin I tumbled on to my bed of sheepskins, exhausted. Throughout the walk I had done nothing but silently curse the old swindler, as I stumbled my way under the weight of my heavy burden. I hadn't been in a fit state to think through any strategies. Now, on the other hand, I had a whole night, a whole long night during which Grock's snoring would help me stay awake and from which I would not emerge without a clear idea, a perfect plan, an ingenious ruse to put an end to my humiliating, forced submission. It was still not dark and I passed the time staring at the uneven walls, the spiders' webs in the corners, the cracks in the ceiling. At one point as I scanned the room I saw Grock's head, leaning against the chimney and I immediately looked away. I stared at the ceiling again (I counted five cracks, six damp patches and a significant drip) and looked down one of the walls. Some of the stones suggested curious, amusing shapes: a Chinese pagoda, a bell tower, a miniature village inhabited by jolly little creatures, or maybe it was a festive lunch in the countryside? I avoided looking at the chimney breast and my gaze came to rest in a corner of the room. Despite my aching back, which demanded that I stayed perfectly still, I sat up and took a closer look, instantly forgetting all about imaginary villages full of little creatures and merry post-prandial dances in the countryside. There, on a shelf, swollen with damp and covered in dust after years of neglect, was a book. Seized with emotion, I went to pick it up and read: Holy Bible. Someone, beside me, made a sharp violent movement and I understood, without taking my eyes off the book, that Grock had stopped fiddling with the fire and had jumped to his feet. 'Mother,' he bleated. 'My mother.'

I was too familiar with the crofter's language by now to be disconcerted by his strange outpourings. No, what I was holding in my hands was not some rustic box, a crude imitation of a book, in which my unpredictable despot might have kept his mother's ashes; nor did it even occur to me that the illiterate old man was stark raving mad and thought that he'd been engendered by a mouldy old volume which I had indiscreetly dared to remove from its resting place. That book was nothing more or less than a book. And Grock, when he referred to his progenitor, was merely letting me know, in his peculiar way, that the Bible had belonged to his mother or that, possibly, it was the only memento he still had of her. I opened it at the first page and knowing, from experience, that the old man's impregnable brain could produce the strangest outbursts at any time, I hastened to focus his attention. 'It's a Bible,' I said, then I started to read:

'In the beginning God created the heaven and the earth. And the earth was without form, and void; and darkness was upon the face of the deep. And the Spirit of God moved upon the face of the waters. And God said, "Let there be light". . .'

Grock had sat down again next to the fire and was listening to me enthralled, without blinking, as if he were in the presence of a marvel, or a delightful vision. I wondered whether that coarse crofter was capable of understanding anything I was reading to him, or whether the reason for his sudden state of enchantment was purely the power of those words. I read some more verses of Genesis until the darkness and cold forced me to take a seat next to the fireplace. Every trace of authority or fury had disappeared from Grock's face. He looked like a child again, a defenceless child, immobilised by wonderment, urging me by his silence not to interrupt my magical reading for anything in the world. I continued:

'And God said, "Let the earth bring forth the living creature . . . and fowl that may fly above the earth in the open firmament of heaven . . ." '

And I noticed that the old man was nodding his head now and again and his eyes were shining from the very centre of each of his pupils. Grock had heard that story before. Probably when he was small, sitting next to a similar fire and from the mouth of a woman who knew how to disentangle the strange marks (the same ones that Grock was now scrutinising over my shoulder) and convert them, as if by magic, into powerful, harmonious words. In a fleeting and almost imperceptible gesture of affection, the crofter's rough hand seemed to become soft as it touched my hair. He looked agitated and shaky and I was concerned that he might burst into tears (as he had done on previous occasions) at the memory of something that, like everything that made him emotional, had happened 'long time ago.' On this occasion, to my relief, his display of emotion consisted of a couple of sighs and a few drops of saliva which I stoically received on one of my ears.

Convinced that what really fascinated the old man was the ritual itself, the prodigious art of reading, I indulged myself by interrupting the thread of a few stories, repeating certain passages and selecting fragments at whim, which I recited in a clear, measured voice by the light of the fire. I went from Genesis to Joshua, from Esther to Proverbs and, with a strange shudder, I settled on Daniel. I didn't give any thought either to the prophet or to the number of times that, in different circumstances and other languages, I had read those pages. Simply coming across my own name written in typeset letters gave me a jolt. 'Daniel,' I said to myself, and I repeated it until I convinced myself that the first word that I had learned to sketch out, long before actually learning how to write, really belonged to me. I read:

'In the third year of the reign of king Belshazzar a vision appeared even unto me, Daniel . . .'

I became lost in my thoughts again, astonished that those six letters which spelled out my first given name in the eyes of my family and the world, could have shared my life for so many years only to abandon me, almost without trace, as soon there was no longer any need for me to be identified in the presence of my family and the world. 'Maybe,' I said in the same tone as I had read the Sacred Scriptures, 'the first thing that a human being forgets is his own given name.' Grock's fetid breath was now breathing down the back of my neck and reminded me that I was not the only one suffering misfortune. I smiled at him and, being as friendly as I could, I suggested that he abandoned his uncomfortable position on my shoulder and sit back down on the chair and that, in order to listen to such wonderful stories, he didn't need to follow the strange marks on the paper that it was beyond his power to understand. Once liberated from his stifling proximity, I continued:

'Then I lifted up mine eyes, and saw, and, behold, there stood before the river a ram which had two horns: and the two horns were high, but one was higher than the other, and the higher came up last.

I saw the ram pushing westward, and northward, and southward; so that no beasts might stand before him, neither was there any that could deliver out of his hand; but he did according to his will and became great.

And as I was considering, behold, an he-goat came from the west on the face of the whole earth . . . and the he-goat had a notable horn between his eyes.

And he came to the ram that had two horns, which I had seen standing before the river, and ran unto him in the fury of his power.

And I saw him come close unto the ram, and he was moved with choler against him, and smote the ram and brake his two horns; and there was no power in the ram to stand before him, and he cast him down to the ground, and stamped upon him: and there was none that could deliver the ram out of his hand.

Therefore the he-goat waxed very great and when he was strong, the great horn was broken; and for it came up four notable ones toward the four winds of heaven.'

Reading that passage made me feel very uneasy. I skipped a few verses and, wanting to draw the evening to a close, I concluded,

'And I Daniel fainted, and was sick certain days; afterward I rose up, and did the king's business; and I was astonished at the vision, but none understood.'

I closed the book suddenly and placed it back on the shelf. The story I'd just read out was enormously similar to my own life, too similar for me not to consider it an omen, a portent from the gods or, at the very least, a simple coincidence with which an implacable, cunning Destiny had once again enjoyed confronting me with my own strange fate. But I was not the only one to be impressed. Grock, beside me, kicked his feet in the air with pleasure, like a schoolboy insisting on his favourite story being read out to him again and again, or like an absolute ruler indisposed to permit his subjects to neglect the smallest detail of his affairs. And Grock's affairs demanded my active participation right then: to keep on telling the story about the ram and the he-goat until I was blue in the face, to stop at the same point at which I had interrupted my reading the first time, and laugh with him when, shaking on his crude chair, he couldn't manage to say anything except, 'Grock, Grock, Grock . . .' and point at the book. My coarse crofter looked upon that passage as if it were his private property. He recognised the ram, enjoyed his submission to the he-goat and revelled in the state of prostration to which the prophet was reduced after the vision. I didn't pause to consider whether the old man saw himself in the role of heroic rescuer, identified with the he-goat or if he simply remembered the great shock that my first encounter with the bloodthirsty sheep had given me. The only thing I was sure of was that his isolation from the world made him react in a completely different way to me. In all likelihood, the last thing in the world that Grock would forget was his own name.

When I felt exhausted after so much re-reading and so much hilarity, I realized that I no longer had to spend the whole night racking my brains for the miraculous ruse that I referred to earlier. In just a few hours, my situation had turned around significantly and from now on, if Grock wanted me to do him any favours, he would have no option but to contain his boundless appetite for control. The revelation that, for different reasons, each of us needed the other, filled me with hope. So I called an end to the evening's activities and was lulled to a gentle sleep by my companion's hoarse breathing. The next day, I told him I intended to return to the shelter. Grock agreed with a grumble, but he filled a bag with his best cheeses and some bits of dried meat and handed it to me.

From slave to personal assistant; from castaway to Shahrazad; but to tell the truth I could not stop grinning about my promotion.

14

For several days I enjoyed the priceless pleasure of being all by myself, alone. I cleared the remains of the slaughtered sheep from my lair, lit a good fire and started to read through my manuscript. I was amazed that, while I was ill, it hadn't occurred to Grock to consign the pages to a speedy end in the heat of the flames. I rewrote a few passages and added some others, recorded the latest events and, all the while, I felt convinced that those pages were going to serve as a record of this extraordinary adventure for someone else, rather than just for me.

My hypothetical reader, originally faceless, had been slowly acquiring physical features and characteristics. He would be more or less my age, twenty-four, twenty-seven, maybe thirty years old; he would suffer my misfortunes along with me and be happy when things went well. The fact that I assumed he was intelligent and well-educated was incentive enough for me to try to keep my descriptions as concise as possible, so as not to succumb to the vice of stating the obvious, and (now that the spectre of madness had disappeared) I restricted myself to noting down the daily news, like a business diary or collection of telegraph messages. It was a great idea. Because my friendly, accommodating reader gave me, from his remote outpost, enough company and support for me to hope for the imminent arrival of my rescue.

However, much as I tried to savour the delights of my newly regained solitude, I couldn't stop thinking about the old crofter. I was surprised by his reverential respect for the written word: by the fact that he had kept that old tome with the mouldy covers for years and years, on the warped, dusty shelf, and his fortunate inaction in regard to the yellowing pages which comprised my precious manuscript. I was also amazed at the sudden terror he'd displayed when I made my incursion into the gloomy forest of shadows, and his refusal to enter that part of his dominions. I wrote:

'Grock, in his isolation, needs to believe in Something superior, whom he can venerate, respect and fear. His range of movement across the island is absolute, apart from a lugubrious, lifeless forest which he won't enter for anything in the world. The forest is his god, and the crofter is convinced that, as long as he doesn't encroach beyond the first line of trees, the forest, his god, will allow him to continue enjoying his immense privileges: ruling over these rocky, foggy lands, controlling the flocks of sheep and rams, and gathering, without too much effort, firewood and provisions.'

And I resolved that I would develop this idea later on. But I didn't get round to it. Because, although it was true that what I looked upon as hell on earth was absolute heaven for Grock, it didn't seem wise to indulge my imagination and allow myself to create such a tale (or indeed any other) with that poor simpleton as the central character. But the truth is that something about those fanciful thoughts had struck a chord in my mind. Every time I went to the hollow to collect timber and firewood I avoided looking towards the forest. I'm not sure whether it was because of the feeling of death it had given off on the first day or out of respect for the crofter's strange qualms.

Grock needed me, as I had suspected. This was confirmed to me with irritating speed, when I was engrossed in writing and entertaining myself with the thought of how my (now indispensable) reader would react to the report of my latest adventures. The old man was not bothered by the cold or hailstones. He'd made the journey to my sheepfold soaked to the skin, hiding something inside his sheepskin, which it wasn't too hard for me to identify and which he immediately held out to me with a wavering smile. His arrival at that point was inconvenient and I tried to make him understand that. But Grock kept patting me on the back, insistently, urging me to open the book with the mouldy covers which he had carefully protected against the storm, and I knew I was doomed to go back over the passage in the Book of Daniel which had given so much pleasure to my listener and which I was starting to think of as a torture.

Resigned to the inevitable I closed the ink bottle and gathered up my papers. I fancied that the crofter gave them a reproachful look, as if his savage instincts let him sense the presence of a human being, to whom he didn't have access, who was intruding in our relationship as a rival. At the end of the day, the old man was right. Grock had saved my life. Now my reader, from his remote outpost, was going to save me from Grock's coarseness.

That night and on other nights too, I tried unsuccessfully to dazzle my companion with the destruction of Babylon, Joshua's dreams or the wealth of the queen of Sheba. Grock's preferences remained unchanged and I had no choice but to accommodate him and regulate, for once and for all, the frequency of our neighbourly relations. Every third night I would visit the crofter's home, do my reading duties and sleep on the sheepskins stretched out on the floor. In exchange, he would provide me with food and firewood, and would respect my days of solitude. Unless of course some important event occurred on the island (such as the arrival of the 'Men from Glasgow'), in which case he should warn me as soon as possible. Grock agreed through clenched teeth and shot another mistrustful look at my manuscript. The thought that he was jealous made me smile but, at the same time, fearful of his outbursts. That was how, with the simple idea of keeping him occupied, I found myself saying without much conviction, 'I need some boards and timbers in the largest possible sizes. Can you get some them for me?' The crofter shrugged his shoulders and looked at me questioningly. 'I'm going to build a raft,' I added mechanically, and then I realized that what I'd just ad-libbed was actually not a bad idea. A raft to keep Grock entertained during the day and, who knew whether, later on, it might bring forward the date of my liberation.

That happy thought kept me occupied for several weeks. The old man, tied up in the search (but never forgetting my reciprocal obligation every third evening) became a sociable and obliging neighbour. Neither of us had the faintest clue how to set about the task. I drew several sketches of rudimentary boats on a sheet of paper and showed them to my assistant to see what he thought, and we ended up, invariably, putting aside such fanciful projects and applying ourselves to nailing together planks in a way which, at that time, seemed easiest and most secure. What had started as a game ended up becoming a real obsession. I thought that the raft was the most ingenious project that any human being had ever embarked upon throughout history and, long before it could be considered finished, I decided to carry out the first trial. Grock politely offered to drag it to the sea and, for such a momentous event, I chose a small pebble beach not far from the cliff I had been brought to by the now nearly forgotten *Providence*.

It was cold and visibility was still practically zero. Nevertheless, I draped the remaining shreds of the life jacket over the red bomber jacket, which I never took off, sang *In taberna* for old times' sake and was gripped with the certainty that I was closing the circle of a whole series of hardships which, not very long afterwards, even I would find hard to believe.

After the third attempt I began to lose confidence in the maritime qualities of my raft. That boat-building project was determined to confront me with the impenetrable mysteries of the laws of buoyancy. It let in water through the joints between the trunks, turned round and round like a spinning top and invariably submerged completely as soon as I tried to use some handles to drag myself on top of its rough and bumpy surface. I didn't try a fourth time. I was brutally separated from my unmanageable invention by a large wave and I ended up being dashed against a rocky outcrop, in a position curiously similar to the one I remembered on the day I woke up on the island. The circle, which I had so ingeniously attempted to close, was turning into a whirlpool.

I shrugged my shoulders. I cursed the admirable skills displayed by castaways and heroes from the past in several languages. I damned to hell every single author of adventure stories, without any exception whatsoever. I cursed Grace and Yasmine . . . Where would they be now? Why had they got me out of the way so easily, writing me off as dead? Had they held a lavish funeral for me? Did they even have the faintest idea about how awful my life had become? I didn't bother to salvage the remnants of the raft. A violent, persistent wind was now competing with the strength of the waves in a clear attempt to make me lose my balance. It was as if the forces of nature were conspiring, once again, to rub my nose in how trivial I was. But the wind, I recalled, sweeps some things away and sweeps other, different things back in. And not just the wind. Because I suddenly realized that the fog was clearing from time to time and that something, bobbing along on the crest of the waves, seemed to be giving me signals and signs and only I could see this. I was struck by the strange feeling that, in its own way, the sea wanted to speak to me, and I stayed there watching for quite some time as first some letters, then some words, a message (try as I might, I couldn't quite decipher it in full), bobbed in and out of sight. When the final wave hurled a wooden board at my feet I crouched down and, seized by a growing nervousness, I brushed the sand and seaweed off the surface.

It was nothing more than a warning to intruders; a sign which suggested that there would be dozens of other signs the length and breadth of that misty, shadowy island; a warning that suddenly made me understand the reason for the fenced-off beaches, the barbed wire, the boats that never thought to stop near a cursed island. Finally, I understood why the crofters had left, why my sheepfold was abandoned who knew how long ago. I read:

GRUINARD ISLAND
DANGER OF CONTAMINATION
NO ENTRY

Once again, I felt the distressing impotence of being a prisoner. But I couldn't give up. I looked up to the heavens to unleash my wrath against the Almighty and, at the same time, desperately plea for a miracle. For a moment, my eyes clouded over and I wanted to believe that someone very much like God the Father had taken pity on my fate and was making an appearance in the very centre of hell. But, when I dried my tears, the vision disappeared. The only people there were the two of us. Me, with my fist raised against the heavens and Grock, at the top of the cliff, jumping up and down and laughing like a child.

15

When the fog had almost completely cleared and, for the first time, I could see a panoramic view of my surroundings, I realized that the recently christened Gruinard was very similar to Grock's Island, with one minor exception which disconcerted me and which, at first, I put down to my terrible sense of direction.

I had not been mistaken in describing the island as rocky and inhospitable or in suspecting that, apart from what I already knew, very little or nothing at all would actually be revealed on that much-anticipated and longed-for day. However, now that I was entertaining myself by locating my points of reference from the top of a hill, I couldn't help being amazed at the unusual topography. The forest, for example, was quite a lot closer to my shelter than I had always thought, and the same could be said for the spring and the esplanade where, some time ago now, I had come across the stinking sheep as they were engaged in one of their bloodthirsty pastimes. I scanned the path up to the crossroads, continued up a hill and followed along a track but, however much I strained my eyes, I could not make out the crofter's hut. As a whole, Gruinard's appearance seemed to lack all logic. Or was it simply a curious optical illusion? When, suddenly, I located a smoking chimney at a ridiculously close distance, I realized that Gruinard was just a smaller version of Grock's Island and that the old man was largely responsible for my humiliating deception.

Because there was my unusual neighbour's place of abode, less than a stone's throw away. He was an old swindler who, taking advantage of the persistent fog, had deliberately given me a distorted view of his estate, leading me along ridiculously roundabout paths, using my total ignorance to protect his authority. Grock's estate. It was nothing more than a silly little island where I had begun to feel weighed down by a stifling sense of immensity. I felt more stupid than ever. Grock had a childish cunning and I remembered myself and my sister Grace, in the long-distant days of our childhood, dividing our playroom up into imaginary paths which everyone who dared enter our territory was obliged to respect. Our dominions, like Grock's, were vast and unassailable.

I didn't get seriously angry. In fact, I didn't have time to get angry or to take two strides over to the crofter's house and return the joke. There was an encouraging sense of clarity opening up before me which I decided to enjoy down to the last second. I ran down to the sea, made out a blurred outline which I guessed was the nearest coast and, armed with an infinite patience, I stayed there for two days waving my bomber jacket at anything that looked like the faintest suspicion of the shape of a boat. On the morning of the third day, the clearest morning since I had set foot on the island, I could see clearly how close we were to the coast and I realized, with a certain embarrassing astonishment, that I was in a much busier place than I could have ever imagined in my moments of greatest euphoria. That afternoon, finally, a pleasure boat came close enough for me to understand that my cries for help had been noticed.

How could I get annoyed with Grock's mischief now that the whole nightmare was about to draw to a close? How could I blame him for not recognizing Gruinard's name and for not being able to explain to me the meaning of that strange warning sign which referred to 'no entry' and 'contamination'? Two days later, to the crofter's terror and my indescribable delight, a helicopter flew over the island.

The helicopter never landed. It hovered in the air just a few metres above me as I waved my arms around. To my complete and utter surprise, one of the men on board shouted down at me through a megaphone: 'What on earth do you think you're doing here?'

I could never have imagined that before being rescued I would have to undergo an exhaustive questionnaire. They asked me how I had arrived on the island, how long I had spent there, who I was, what was my profession . . . They sounded curt and business like, with a trace of distaste which they didn't trouble to hide, as if they found their mission highly disagreeable or they were in the presence of someone who'd committed a crime. The man with the megaphone broke off from his interrogation for a few moments and whispered something in the pilot's ear. But they didn't lower any ladders or ropes. 'Listen carefully,' they said.

Yes, I knew. I was on Gruinard, a name that I began to detest even more than Grock's Island, a place where the land was contaminated and they weren't going to be able to rescue me right then. In exactly seven days' time a launch would land on one of the beaches, under instructions from a team of scientists. Until then they had to take certain precautions and I, for my part, should strictly adhere to a course of medication. They threw down a bag containing food and medicine. Inside I found the instructions which I had to read and follow to the letter. Seven days, that was all. They asked me to stay calm but, above all (and here the man in the uniform's voice sounded deadly serious) I had to refrain from making any sort of signal to passing ships. My case, they said, was being monitored.

I picked up the bag with as much resignation as I could muster and looked back up at them. 'One more thing,' said the man with the megaphone. 'It's unlikely but possible that you'll meet (if you haven't already met) an old crofter, who's reclusive and violent. Don't get too close to him. He's dangerous and . . . he's also contaminated.' Before flying off, the helicopter spun round on itself and a third man, who I hadn't noticed before, pointed a camera at me and took a photograph.

It was all so strange, so formal, so cold and bureaucratic, that I stood there for a long while, next to the bag of provisions, watching spellbound as the machine manoeuvred through the air.

I found Grock where I'd left him, hiding in my cabin, with a look of surprise still etched on his face. I opened the bag and read the instruction sheet which was wrapped around some medicine bottles and a couple of packets of pills. At the bottom I found some tins, concentrated food, fruit juice, coffee, cigarettes, matches . . . 'Don't go near Grock,' I remembered. But I wasn't prepared to comply with the last item on the prescription. That afternoon we had a party by the heat of the fire, and the same the next day, and the next. When we got to the fourth day, the provisions had run out and we went back to our usual diet based on seaweed, fish and sheep's cheese. Now, at nightfall, the sky was full of stars and you could see the lights along the coast. In the morning, sitting on the top of the cliff, I would contemplate how close we were to civilization and a shudder went through my whole body. Without any doubt, they were the longest seven days since I had arrived on the island, during which I contained my impatience by telling Grock things that he couldn't understand. What a helicopter was, what the pills were for, where the country I was from was located. By now my photograph would have appeared in all the papers and, in a very short while, the rescue team (scientists, he'd said) would come for me in a launch. Were they the same people who brought the bottles for Grock? Was he, in some capacity, the island's guard? The crofter listened to me without blinking, reluctant to leave my side, still shocked by the unearthly appearance of that contraption he had probably been unaware of until then. On the final evening, he looked so sad and taciturn that I resolved to offer him a symbolic token of my gratitude. I gave him the captain's red bomber jacket and he, as happy as a sandboy, insisted on me wearing his sheepskin jacket.

That night neither of us could sleep. For my part, because I was counting down the minutes to my rescue; Grock, because he must have known that, the following day, he was going to lose his only friend.

16

When I opened my eyes and saw Grock with his ears pricked up like an animal in a state of heightened alert, I realized that sleep must have got the better of me despite my nerves, and that my companion's sharp hearing must have picked up the sound of a launch in the distance. I sat up with a start and shouted, 'It's them!' and the next second, before I could work out what was going on, I was hurtling against one of the walls.

The old man looked at me with an expression that defied description. He was holding the Bible which I was so familiar with in one hand and in the other he brandished a thick rope, which he waved in the air in a menacing way. He grunted something that I didn't manage to decipher, threw me against the wall again and tied the rope around my waist with prodigious speed and skill, stifling my protests by hitting me with the Sacred Scriptures and tying me to one of the rocks which, on previous nights, we had used as a table for our extended farewell party. I shouted and pleaded to no avail. Grock bounded out of the door and, dragging myself pitifully along the floor, I only managed to glimpse a flash of red as he disappeared behind one of the hills.

Luckily, the same element of surprise that had impeded my reactions had also led the crofter to underestimate my strength. Drawing on all my energy I managed to free myself from the heavy rock and, knowing that I had no time to lose, I wound the rest of the rope around my waist and started off along the path to the coast, crouching and hiding among the rocks. Now I knew that Grock wasn't willing to return to the solitude he had known before he met me, and I didn't doubt that he would be capable of using much blunter means if he discovered me away from my shelter. After a while, I hid behind a rock and watched. Six men had landed on Gruinard and were advancing quickly towards the centre of the island. I was about to wave my arms and call out, now that I was finally in the presence of my rescuers, when I heard a shout and I saw Grock leaping out from among the rocks and running towards them in leaps and bounds. Then something happened that absolutely petrified me, as I watched from my hiding place.

Three of the six men had just pulled out their guns and pointed them at the crofter. Then everything happened too quickly for me to do anything to stop it. Immediately after the sound of gunshots, there was a cry of pain. Grock's arms went up in the air and he took a few steps forward. There were more gunshots and the old man fell flat on his face on to the rocks, never to get up again.

For a good while I stayed where I was, dumbfounded, watching the movements of those men whose voices were carried to me on the wind. I noticed that there had been three more men crouched behind the ones that had fired the shots, as if they totally disagreed with what they had just witnessed or didn't want to be part of what had just taken place a few moments before. They weren't wearing uniforms and they looked very busy collecting soil samples, labelling them and putting them into small tubes which they immediately placed in a metal briefcase. Meanwhile, the first three set about burying Grock in a brutal, disrespectful manner, heaping soil and rocks on top of my companion in misfortune, ostentatiously holding their noses and complaining about the stench from that inert body, which they treated like so much carrion, detritus, debris . . . My stupor had given way to anger but, rather than compel me to action, it left me paralysed. As if in a dream, I watched those murderers as they went about their business. Now the men with the metal briefcase walked towards the forest, accompanied by one of the men in uniform. The others waited next to the mound of earth covering Grock, smoking cigarettes as if they had just completed a dangerous mission and were rewarding themselves with a short breather. Their attitude wrenched at my heartstrings. But they were still brandishing their weapons and I wouldn't have dared let them know I was there until the rest of the team returned. I waited for several long hours, wondering why they had killed my friend. It was true that Grock's appearance was enough on its own to make the bravest man jump out of his skin, and it was highly likely that those men knew only too well about his bouts of violence and interpreted his welcoming charge as an attack. But I found it hard to understand the scientists' indifference, why the men in uniform hadn't even bothered to shout a warning, take precautions, use their superior force over a poor old crofter who wasn't even carrying a weapon. All I could do was to control my anger and wait. No doubt the scientists were busy looking for me.

Another gunshot coming from the forest put an end to the occasional banter between the two security guards. They looked at each other, shrugged their shoulders and, for a moment, remained alert and ready for action. I crouched down even lower. Something was happening on the island which was completely beyond my comprehension. Now, one of the men in uniform started whistling monotonously and the other, as if sensing my presence, passed the time throwing pebbles against the rock I was hiding behind. All of a sudden the whistling stopped, a final pebble bounced over my head and I heard voices and footsteps. One of the security guards asked in a loud voice, 'Everything OK?'

It didn't take long for the reply to come from along the path to the forest and I understood, to my relief, that the exploration party was returning.

'A sheep. It was just a sheep.'

The moment had come to show myself. I waited until the footsteps had mingled with the security guard's reinvigorated whistling, checked that all six men were finally there in front of me, then I jumped on top of the rock and, unable to hold it in for a moment longer, I started shouting at the top of my voice.

Their surprise at my sudden appearance only lasted a few seconds. Three guns were immediately trained on me and the scream stuck in my throat, my eyes clouded over and, at breakneck speed, I froze as a series of vignettes from my own life flashed in front of my eyes.

I didn't have time to be surprised. There I was playing with my sister; there was the seminary cloister; all the places I would never see again; a particular doubt in a certain translation from Aristophanes; Grace's perfume; the taste of hot chocolate on a winter's afternoon; that translation query again; Yasmine's furrowed brow; 'bow-sprit', 'binnacle' and 'hawser'. But I felt no nostalgia or sorrow. At the back of my eyes, which were closed, other images struggled to get through. These were no longer memories or experiences, but images glimpsed in dreams, dreams about dreams, the same reiterations of my dreams.

I realized that I was in death's antechamber and that very soon the dizzy merry-go-round of images would give way to a beatific clarity, a peaceful, regenerative, secretly yearned-for rest. Or maybe I'd been dead for some time, since the very day the *Providence* had run aground on the island. Now I began to understand that Gruinard must be Purgatory and Grock my eccentric jailer. A prison guard who had just enacted a symbolic finale to his mission in order to prepare me to enter into the knowledge, into total rest. But, suddenly, a voice which didn't come from inside me shouted an order. It said, 'Halt!' And all I could do was open my eyes and feel the drama of being alive again.

The men in uniform had lowered their guns and the man with the metal briefcase was standing there with his arm raised, staring at me. After a few moments' thought, he took a few paces towards the rock and, in a measured voice, enunciating each syllable phlegmatically, as if talking to an idiot or someone who was deaf and dumb, he asked, 'Is there anyone else on the island?'

It took me a while to respond and shake my head. My day of liberation was turning out too bizarrely for me to know what I should do or how I should respond. The man said something else in the same tone as his first question, something I didn't understand at first or which my astonishment prevented me from understanding. Then, turning to the rest of the group, he said, 'It's Grock. He's as

133

simple and harmless as a child.'

And, speechless with emotion, I stood motionless on the rock and watched as my supposed rescuers walked off, until I clearly heard the rumble of the launch. Not a sound came from my mouth. Because, if I was Grock, the simple, reclusive crofter who wouldn't leave his dominions for anything in the world, the person buried under that mound of earth and stones couldn't be anyone else but Daniel.

For a second time, the old man had saved my life.

17

I knew straight away what I had to do. I dug up my companion's body, loaded him on my shoulder and headed across the fields towards what, until a few hours earlier, had been his home. The path was long and difficult, almost as difficult as when, ages ago now, Grock had led me to his cabin for the first time, using all sorts of roundabout routes, and I couldn't stop thinking that my friend was insisting on one last macabre demonstration of the vastness of his dominions from beyond the grave. The corpse had become as hard as a rock and, every now and then, I had to place it on the ground and have a rest. During one of those forced breaks I noticed the transformation that had taken place in his face. His features had become very sharp and his skin had acquired the texture of cardboard and the colour of wax. I loaded him on my shoulder again. That distressing reproduction of my friend was becoming unbearable.

When I arrived at the door to his house, just like on another occasion, a long time ago, I collapsed in a heap. But I didn't have any time to lose. I found a pick and a shovel, dug up the soil and nestled Grock's body together with what I surmised were the remains of his best friend. Then I crossed his arms over his chest and covered his now unfamiliar face with earth. Now Grock became once again the Grock I remembered, and I would pray for him and only for him.

But either I couldn't or didn't know how to pray. A voice which sprang from my own throat, emanating from some strange source, recited my farewell. I heard myself declare, 'And, behold, there stood before the river a ram . . .' And I stood there listening to myself, spellbound, imagining that, beneath the earth, those closed eyes had come back to life and were smiling at me now, tired but happy, for repeating his favourite story once more: the confrontation between the he-goat and the ram, and the prostration of the poor, bewildered Daniel. Was that me? Was I the prophet? No, Daniel lay beneath the earth, there at my feet. He was wearing the Captain's red bomber jacket, the same one I was wearing when the men from the helicopter first spotted me, the one that must have been in the photograph that wasn't going to appear in any newspaper, that would never be made public. But there was still one thing that wasn't clear. If a brightly coloured piece of clothing was enough to identify an intruder, it meant that my appearance must have been barely different from that of wild old Grock. I didn't have a mirror to look at myself. But I carried on throwing earth over that body, marked by the terrible hand of death and, for the first time, I realized that I was deformed and monstruous. Because when Daniel died I immediately became Grock, the owner of the island, the simpleton who could be managed with a few bottles of alcohol, the guinea pig for who knows what unspeakable experiments. When I finished off the burial by positioning the cross, I started to laugh and cry like a madman. Just like Grock. I couldn't stop telling myself, 'this is what Grock would have done.' And I stayed there, embracing the earth that covered my great companion, until fatigue overcame my exhilaration and I fell into a deep sleep.

When I woke up dawn was breaking and I was still mouthing the words, 'and the he-goat waxed very great . . .' I rubbed my eyes, sat up and noticed with a start that half a dozen or so of those revolting animals had spent the night with me, as if I were their shepherd and they were calm, docile sheep. An infernal scream issued from my mouth. Seized with a sudden panic, they sped off in all directions.

There was no longer any doubt. The sheep also thought that I'd turned into Grock.

The man who had saved my life by uttering the word, 'Halt!', hadn't hesitated to tell me, 'We don't have enough time for you today, but there on the beach you'll find what you've been waiting for.' And he hadn't been lying. A wooden crate with my ration of whisky and brandy. What I else did I expect? 'We don't have enough time for you today, Grock.' What could I care now? The alternative was clear. There was no point in believing that I was myself any more, in trying to build a new raft or swim to the coast. The only place for Daniel in this world was a dark, damp patch of earth. Grock, on the other hand, was allowed the blessing of life. In a couple of years, the scientists would return. Maybe, then, they'd have more time for me, analyse my pustules, admire my strength and agility, give me a meticulous examination and discover to their amazement how the effect of contamination had produced a spect-acular rejuvenation in the old savage's joints. And I'd have to be careful to imitate the crofter's voice, delight in letting myself be photographed, grab the photo and laugh like a lunatic at what I saw, without letting them know that I was laughing at myself. Because maybe the laughter would be real and delirious amusement would be my only reaction to my own monstruous appearance. Or perhaps events would turn out differently. Two years was a long time. Some ship might smash against the cliff in the middle of winter and a castaway might get lost in the fog and repeat my cycle of hope and suffering. And then, in a ritual ceremony, I would decide to sacrifice myself on behalf of a new Grock. Because perhaps that's what had occurred on the island since the time when its inhabitants were forced to abandon it and my predecessor was nothing more than a simple link in a long chain of Grocks whose story, now, I would have no option but to adopt as mine. Yes, the alternative was clear. To become the Prospero of Gruinard, an illustrious Grock lying in wait for prospective new castaways, a crafty savage capable of interrogating the scientific expedition in multiple languages, singing to them in Latin, insulting them in Greek. I could also dare to do what Grock had never dared. I could go into the forest, search for the tree of knowledge and eat its fruit. The worst thing that could happen would be expulsion from Paradise. Yes, and it must be in the forest where the Supreme Power which petrified my dear Grock resided. All I had to do was believe in it one hundred per cent, act like a lunatic and finally achieve the old crofter's simple happiness: to reign over the dominions I'd inherited and discover the secrets and mysteries of these lands which no mortal, apart from Grock, had the privilege to enjoy.

Now I knew, (and it didn't distress me), that I would never finish the story of my travels in Grace's comfortable home. The time had come to face the real adventure, the one that no one could have predicted, the one which I was not going to bother making a record of, now that my distant, impossible, fastidious reader's face had disappeared.

18

But, once again, as so often in my life, things didn't turn out as I had prophesized. I stayed a few days in the heart of the forest waiting for a revelation that didn't appear and trying to convince myself that a new religion would shortly be born in that lost, damned place on Gruinard, of which, in all likelihood, I was going to be the chief minister and only follower. But I was still not mad enough to convince myself of anything, and nor did the fast which I undertook, in the hope of speeding up events, change my surroundings and regale me with some delightful hallucination on which to base my future beliefs. When hunger started to provoke sharp pangs in my stomach, I gave up my state of contemplation in the lifeless forest and, disappointed, went to my shelter and gorged myself on a couple of cheeses. Afterwards I sat on the top of the cliff and realized, quite satisfied, that for the first time since my arrival on the island I had managed not to think about anything and to feel, at the same time, moderately relaxed and happy. That was when I saw them.

They had just got off a launch, were carrying some bags over their shoulders, and they looked all around them as if they didn't know which path to take to enter into my dominions. They weren't carrying any weapons and they seemed quite young. Their appearance didn't alarm me and, suddenly excited by this unexpected development, I forgot about my own. My hair was dirty and tangled, hanging over my shoulders, I was wearing my predecessor's coarse sheepskin, and the thick rope which the crofter had tried to tie me up with was still hanging from my waist, like a tail. I waved my arms and shouted at the top of my voice. They retreated in terror.

But they had no reason to be afraid of me and, seeing how shocked they were, I didn't bother with any precautions. I went down the cliff as quickly and fearlessly as a goat and, when I got to within a few paces of them, with the sole intention of reassuring them, I forgot about my pretensions of being the absolute ruler of the island and told them I had once been a castaway. After a few moments' hesitation, they told me who they were. They were ecologists and had come to the island, even though it was banned, in order to obtain some samples of contaminated soil and draw attention to the dangers involved in certain experiments, about which they would later speak in great detail. My presence, however, left their vague plans dangling in the air. I suddenly became a living example of the danger they were intending to expose. I was the most spectacular proof of the aberration that the island of Gruinard represented just a few miles off the bay of the same name.

They took me onto their launch, covered me with their bags and kept a prudent distance, not so much out of fear of potential contagion, but rather, as they later confessed, because my stench was almost more than they could stomach. That was how, with no possessions other than my manuscript, I found myself returning to life at a moment when I had thought myself definitively expelled from its bosom.

'What day is it today?' I asked, motivated by rather more than a simple curiosity. They replied in unison: 'The seventh of July, nineteen eighty-one.'

And while I noted in surprise that it happened to be on that special day that my Year of Grace came to an end, comforted by the purr of the engine, I felt enveloped in a sweet drowsiness, making a point of never looking back behind us. I still don't know if it was in recollection of certain biblical curses, or out of the simple and irrational fear of seeing myself at the top of the cliff, desperately waving a battered red bomber jacket.

Appendix

The history of Gruinard Island is not so different from that of Grock's Island. It is located off the north-west coast of Scotland, less than two kilometres from the bay of the same name, and is part of the Inner Hebrides. In 1941, it was chosen as a test site for biological weapons, for possible use against Germany. The ground was contaminated with anthrax spores and the few inhabitants, mainly crofters, were forced to leave. All that remained on the island were some sheep, abandoned to their fate. Since then, Gruinard has remained shut off from the curiosity of the public and just one scientific expedition is allowed to go, every other year, after being subjected to seven months of tests and vaccinations.

However, in the official history, which I relate below as it was told to me, there is not one single reference to Grock or his tragic ending, which had been decided for me several days earlier in some secret office who knows where. I couldn't deny that my situation had undergone a miraculous turnaround. The group of ecologists, my real rescuers, waited for me to recover (or perhaps get worse) in order to show me off as irrefutable proof of their protests. But the abject specimen of humanity that they intended to display quickly became a presentable human being thanks to the sterling efforts of a team of doctors who were determined to achieve the opposite: to minimize the signs of anthrax, downscale my stay on the island to no more than a few weeks and talk up the physical and moral impact of being a castaway. However, whether it was because the experiments which took place in the 1940s had not been as effective as the scientists suspected or because my own state of health was not as alarming as my rescuers had hoped, it can't be denied that the former had been rash in their decision to eliminate me and the latter in indulging in such extreme euphoria. It was not long before both camps started to become tired of me. The youngsters who had taken my manuscript with such strong convictions (and, they claimed, had been forced to destroy it for reasons of basic hygiene) gave me back a spotless photocopy of the original. They had been unable to translate a single line and (without any great enthusiasm) they asked me, if after deciphering my own handwriting I could find anything that might be of interest to their cause, to send it on to them. On the other hand, one of the doctors (who I felt certain was not just an doctor but had some other role) seemed suspiciously insistent that I was emotionally disturbed and tried to coax out of me any memories which didn't relate to solitude or the difficulties of survival. I didn't make a single allusion to Grock, or to the fate which, consciously or not, he had probably saved me from (at least, that's what I thought at that time) for reasons of strict security.

Before being discharged, with my hearing and eyesight still damaged ('as a result of the shipwreck', naturally) skilled surgeons removed the pustules and erased, as much as possible, the scars of my long stay on Gruinard. It seemed that this was particularly difficult to achieve in the corners of my mouth. They recommended that I grew a moustache and I did what I was told. Then, wearing some glasses with thick pebble lenses, I looked at myself in the mirror for the first time, and smiled at the subtle but significant change in my appearance. However, when I saw one of the photographs they'd taken when I'd been admitted to the hospital, I didn't have the courage to laugh at myself.

I decided to return to Barcelona quietly, get used to the world again and to my new appearance. A week later, I was on the Dover to Calais ferry, trying to sort out my feelings and, for most of the voyage, avoiding a revolting group of rowdy schoolgirls. In one of the lounges, as I was looking at myself in the mirror, still confused, I heard laughter from behind me which had a strange effect on me. I turned around and saw a group of a dozen women with red hair and freckles. Recovering the arrogance of an earlier Daniel, lost in the past, I asked the woman who was laughing what was so funny. She said she didn't know. She said she was just laughing, that she came from Leadburn, near Edinburgh, and that, like the other women, she had won a prize in a competition run by a supermarket chain and she was going to a place called Paris, first, then somewhere else called Barcelona. She showed me a brochure with the highlights of the trip, said her name was Gruda McEnrich and started laughing again because, she explained, the sea made her feel very scared.

I disembarked at Calais and, without really knowing why, I headed for Saint-Malo. I wasn't searching for anything in particular, other than to convince myself that Saint-Malo really did exist and that, months earlier, an extremely young and inexperienced youth had walked along the same quay dreaming about fascinating adventures. I drifted towards a café which I remembered very well, then to a lodging house, and then to another café. That was when, in the last café, that I started to believe in ghosts for the first time in my life.

The café was called *Providence* and there was a picture of Captain Jean smiling down at me from one of the walls. On the other side of the bar, a sallow-faced, middle-aged man in a suit was peevishly serving customers. I had to steady myself against a table in order not to fall over. But Naguib had shown no signs of recognizing me. I sat down next to an old man who was completely drunk and bought him several drinks. We went on from there to another bar, and then another. That's how I found out about the amazing story of the Egyptian's miraculous rescue. Naguib was picked up alive by a merchant ship. And not only was he alive. In one of his life-jacket pockets, carefully protected, was a cheque in his favour for a very large amount, drawn on a bank in Glasgow. It was a story about loyalty and . . . *providence.* The man laughed at his own joke for a minute or so and continued, 'When Captain Jean realized that he couldn't stop the boat from sinking, he refused to abandon ship, wrote out a cheque to the deck hand, told him that was everything he had in the world and said goodbye, wishing him the best of luck. Apparently he told him, "If you manage to survive, enjoy it in my memory." That's a sad story, isn't it?'

I took off my glasses and, for a few seconds, my unsteady companion disappeared in the mist and shadows.

'Yes, it's an incredible story,' was all I said.

But I was not being at all ironic.

That same night I arrived in Paris, slept in the first hotel I could find and, the next day, sat down at one of the tables in the café where, just a few months earlier, I had thought of myself as one whom the gods loved. Everything was painfully the same as I remembered it. The same conversations, the same faces. I felt a strange shiver and, with some trepidation, I asked after Yasmine. The waiter shrugged his shoulders, but he pointed to a shy young man with a slightly gypsy-like appearance. Another ex-seminarian? Or an ex-convict, maybe? With a rush of joy I remembered Gruda and the name of her hotel printed in the brochure. That afternoon, Miss McEnrich and I went to the cinema.

When I got to Barcelona I telephoned my sister, then her agent, and later on her solicitor. Grace was in Venezuela on her second honeymoon with her second husband. I was happy for her. She, on the other hand, according to her solicitor, didn't want to have anything to do with me and my total ingratitude. So I made two decisions. The first was to recount my voyage to the Rector of the Seminary. The second was to marry Gruda. When he heard the tale of my adventures, the Rector couldn't stop laughing. When she heard my proposal of marriage Gruda couldn't contain her surprise. Later, after a while, as I tried to adapt to the bustle of city life, I finally understood the reason for my obstinate silence in the hospital and for my total passivity when I discovered the café called *Providence*. There was a part of my life which I couldn't or didn't want to share. Because, at night, while Gruda tossed and turned in bed, dreaming out loud or breathing heavily, I liked to imagine, in the comfort of the darkness, that I was still a castaway, that my faithful friend was still sleeping beside me and that possibly, when I woke up, I would be back on the calm, peaceful Grock Island.

And then, only then, after indulging in such fond memories, could I fall into an enviably deep sleep or abandon myself to delightfully sweet dreams.

The Clapton Press

Lightning Source UK Ltd.
Milton Keynes UK
UKHW021241080722
405575UK00008B/1600